ACCLAIM FOR THE NOVELS OF SHEILA ROBERTS

"Roberts's witty and effervescently funny novel will warm hearts. Realistic characters populate the pages of this captivating story, which is a great escape from the hustle and bustle."

—*Romantic Times* (Top Pick)

"A beautifully written story that is populated with real and charming people."

—*Fresh Fiction*

"Roberts writes compellingly about the issues faced by women in different stages of life."

—*Booklist*

"Hilarious . . . a fun and festive debut; for all women's fiction collections"

—*Library Journal*

"Roberts's world . . . will doubtless warm more than a few hearts."

—*Publishers Weekly*

"The funny novel is all about love . . . and friendships. But, most of all, it's about learning to love yourself before you can love anyone else."

—*The Columbus Dispatch*

"Roberts manages to avoid genre clichés and crafts a heartfelt novel with nuggets of life truths."

—*The Press & Sun-Bulletin*

THE SNOW GLOBE

ALSO BY SHEILA ROBERTS

THE
SNOW
GLOBE

Sheila Roberts

ST. MARTIN'S PRESS

NEW YORK

THE SNOW GLOBE. Copyright © 2010 by Sheila Rabe. All rights reserved. Printed in the United States of America. For information, address St. Martin's Press, 175 Fifth Avenue, New York, N.Y. 10010.

www.stmartins.com

ISBN 978-0-312-59448-0

First Edition: November 2010

10 9 8 7 6 5 4 3 2 1

FOR ROSEBUD

ACKNOWLEDGMENTS

This was such a fun book to write! Of course it's always fun when you get to work with great people. And I want to take a moment to thank some of them right now. Thanks to my buddy Ruth, for all the great insight and encouragement. Huge thanks to Susan Wiggs, Elsa Watson, and Anjali Banerjee, for keeping an eagle eye on my work in progress. Most of all, thanks to my fabulous agent, Paige Wheeler, and my amazing editor, Rose Hilliard, and all the super people at St. Martin's Press, who worked so hard to help this story become a book. May you all see your dreams come true this Christmas!

ONE

Something drew Kiley Gray to the antique shop. It could have been the carousel horse in the window or the sight of tables and shelves beyond, crammed with cast-off treasures. Whatever was in there calling to her, she knew she had to go in. She was a big believer in that sort of thing.

Actually, Kiley was a big believer, period. She'd been sure Santa was real until she was ten and even after waking up on Christmas Eve to discover her father hanging her filled stocking on the mantel, she kept pretending for another two years. She'd believed in Prince Charming and Mr. Right clear through college. She'd even believed in happy endings until just this past October when her boyfriend Jeremy Horne dumped her at her own Halloween party (how was that for tacky?), announcing that he couldn't fight his attraction for her sister any longer.

It had been a very scary Halloween.

A bell chimed over the door as Kiley entered the shop and her nose twitched as she caught a whiff of dust.

Another shopper, a middle-aged woman in a stylish wool coat, stood at the counter, raving over the pink Depression glass pitcher she'd found. "And just in the nick of time," she added. "I'm going to have to dash to make that ferry." With hurried thanks, she took the piece the shop owner had carefully wrapped and hurried to the door, stuffing bills in her wallet as she went.

One fluttered to the floor and Kiley scooped it up. It was a fifty, maybe not a lot for this woman, who was well dressed and obviously had money to burn, but to Kiley it was a fortune. "Wait. You dropped this."

"Oh. Thanks," said the woman, barely looking at it. She stuffed it in her purse and hurried out the door.

The shopkeeper, a portly man with thinning, gray hair, smiled at Kiley. "People get in too big of a hurry."

"I can't afford to be in *that* big of a hurry," she said. She probably couldn't afford to be in here at all. But browsing didn't cost anything, she told herself as she drifted to where the carousel horse stood frozen in mid-prance. Who had owned this and how had it wound up languishing here? Kiley gave it a comforting pat then wandered past a table overflowing with nautical knick-knacks toward an antique sideboard displaying tarnished silver and faded china, waiting for their glory days to return.

Then she saw something out of the corner of her eye. She turned and moved to the far side of the shop for a closer look. Tucked behind a clock with a brass horse and a chipped crystal vase sat an old snow globe. She might never have noticed it if it hadn't gotten caught by a stray sunbeam that managed to slip past the gray clouds outside and in through the window.

She picked it up, charmed by the scene inside the thick glass: a toyshop in the center of an Alpine village. She gave the globe a shake and watched the snow swirl around the little angel standing guard in front of the shop. It was simply too charming not to buy. Anyway, purchasing treasures was an integral part of any girls' getaway weekend so, in a way, she was almost obligated.

She took it to where the shop owner sat behind his cash register, now reading a book. "I didn't see a price tag on this. I'm just wondering what you want for it."

She gulped when he told her. Not exactly a wise purchase for a girl who had a steady job, let alone one who was now unemployed. Maybe purchasing treasures wasn't such an integral part of a girls' getaway weekend. At least not this treasure, not this weekend. Heck, at that price, never.

The man looked over his reading glasses at her and smiled. "But, I think, for the right buyer, I could come down in price."

Not enough, she was sure. Still, she couldn't resist asking, "What does the right buyer look like?" Hopefully, a skinny woman edging toward thirty with unruly brown hair, hazel eyes, a fashionably full mouth, and a nose she hated.

"It's not exactly about looks," the shop owner said. "It's more about where you are in life. You see, this little snow globe has quite a story to tell."

"I like stories," said Kiley, leaning her elbows on the counter.

"This one starts back when snow globes were first being made. Nobody knows the exact date, but the first one appeared at the Paris Exposition in 1878, and by 1879 at least five companies were producing snow globes and selling them throughout Europe. The woman who brought this to me claims it was one of them, so you can see it's very valuable."

"If it's that valuable I wonder why she didn't take it to *Antiques Roadshow*," Kiley mused. It seemed like the kind of thing that would go for a king's ransom at Sotheby's.

The man nodded his agreement. "She had her reasons. You see, its age isn't the only thing that makes it valuable." He removed his reading glasses and set aside his book. "Would you like to hear more?"

"I'm not in a hurry," said Kiley. "But I hope this story has a happy ending. I'm kind of in need of happy endings these days."

"Are you? Well, you be the judge."

Chicago, December 1880

It had been one year since Otto Schwartz had lost his whole world. And he was still alive, if one could call moving through each day like a ghost living. This particular day he stood at his toyshop window, watching snow carpet the street. Delivery wagons passed, people walked by with paper-wrapped parcels, happily shopping for Christmas.

Two children, a boy and a girl bundled in heavy coats, hats, and mittens, ran ahead of their mother and stopped in front of the shop window to peer at Otto's display of porcelain dolls, tin toys, and stuffed animals. They pressed their faces to the glass and pointed excitedly. One even smiled at Otto. He tried to smile back. A ghost of a smile.

The woman caught up with them, keeping her face averted. Taking the children by the hand, she led them off down the street. He could hardly blame her for not wanting to look at him. His toys called to one and all to step inside and find fun and laughter. But once inside people found Otto and they hurriedly left, recalling more pressing errands.

He watched them walk away and sighed. Children and toys were meant to go together. Men who owned toyshops should have children. And wives.

The sigh became a sob. He turned his back on the snowy Chicago street scene, then dug a handkerchief out of the pocket of his black suit and blew his nose. At least he'd tried to smile.

But the effort was coming late. People expected a man to mourn when he lost his wife and baby—a full year in black and no social engagements (as if he had wanted any)—but they also expected a man to continue to run his business, to set aside his sorrow and take care of his customers. Otto couldn't even care for his own bleeding heart. How could he be expected to care if little Johann would like a wooden marionette or to take an interest in which porcelain doll little Ingrid would want most? At first he had been bereft. He had closed up the shop and shut himself inside his darkened house. Everyone in the city's German community had understood. But finally his sister had shoved Brötchen, sliced ham, and an egg under his nose and commanded that he eat. And that he then go and reopen his shop.

"You are not the first man to lose a wife in childbirth. You will not be the last," she'd said sternly. "Liesel and Gottlieb are in heaven."

"And I am in hell," he had growled, causing his sister to gasp.

She had recovered quickly, shaking a finger at him and retorting, "Then I suggest you crawl out. It is time. You have a business to run."

And so he had gone from bereft to morose, and his friends and neighbors tried to be patient. But when he went from morose to ill-tempered people failed to understand and he lost many a customer. Now Christmas was right around the corner and Otto was trying to remember how to smile. Except that was almost impossible with the snow coming down outside, reminding him of happier times in the village in the Bavarian alps where he had grown up, with people strolling by outside on their way to warm, happy homes.

Peter the mail carrier entered the shop, bringing with him the scent of snow. From somewhere outside the sound of a child's laugh slipped in also, grabbing at Otto's heart.

"Otto, look what I have. Something from your sister in France," Peter called cheerfully, his grin making his moustache dance. If Peter weren't so content with delivering mail he would have made a great diplomat. He was always happy. Even on Otto's grumpiest days Peter entered the shop smiling and left the same way. "Open it and let's see what it is," he suggested. A package from France was worth a five-minute delay in his deliveries.

Otto took the package, carefully unwrapping it and prying

open the wooden box. Nested inside the excelsior he found something more amazing than all the toys in his shop put together.

"What is it?" asked Peter, his voice filled with awe.

"I don't know," said Otto. He picked up the delicate item. It easily fit in the palm of his large hand. A glass globe sat on an ornate ceramic base. Inside it was a nostalgic scene of a toyshop that looked like his father's toyshop on a street in what could have been his village in the Bavarian Alps. Amazing! How had the maker managed that small wonder? The mountains, the snow-capped trees—oh yes, it could have been his village! In front of the toyshop stood a beautiful angel in a white gown with golden hair and blue eyes. She looked just like Liesel. Swallowing the lump in his throat, Otto set the work of art on his counter.

"Those Frenchmen," said Peter, shaking his head in amazement. "What will they think of next?" He motioned to the notepaper still lying in the excelsior. "Read the note and see what it's called."

Otto picked up the paper with trembling fingers and read.

Dear brother,
I know it has been more than a year and you still grieve deeply. Henri commissioned this water globe to be made especially for you in the hope that it would bring you comfort.

"A water globe? Is there water in there?" Peter picked up the globe to examine it.

Otto frowned at him, took the globe from his hand and set it back on the counter, then returned to the letter.

Henri has a friend who makes these in his factory. They are becoming quite popular. They are sometimes called snow globes, a term I much prefer. If you shake it you will see why. Perhaps one day you would like to sell snow globes in your shop. But for now, we want you to have this special one to keep, in memory of your dear Liesel and the baby. Of course, this cannot bring them back, but perhaps it can bring you hope. I have prayed that it will.

Your loving sister, Berthe

"Shake it," urged Peter.

Otto picked up the snow globe and gave it a tentative jiggle.

"Will you look at that!" Peter exclaimed. "I've never seen such a thing in all my life."

Neither had Otto. He stared in amazement as a tiny blizzard swirled around the angel. The snow settled and he shook the globe again, starting a fresh flurry. He wanted to cry. Or laugh. Instead, he smiled.

Peter spread the news of Otto's unusual present throughout the community and soon people were venturing into the store to see the amazing snow globe and ooh and ah over the little scene inside.

"It's lovely," said Mrs. Schmidt. "And the angel reminds me of your wife."

Otto sighed. "Yes, she does." And later that day, after the customers had all left, he couldn't resist holding the thing and gazing inside at the little angel, wishing she could speak to him.

But what was this? The angel's hair, somehow, appeared darker.

Was he imagining it? He shook the globe and started the tiny flakes spinning. Once more they settled at the angel's feet. Her hair still looked darker. Perhaps it had always been dark. Perhaps it had only seemed lighter because of wishful thinking on his part.

Disappointed, he set the snow globe down, wishing it would show him what he wanted to see.

Christmas was two weeks away when a man and woman entered the store. Strangers. Except with her dark hair and sweet smile the woman wasn't a stranger. Otto realized he had seen her before, inside the snow globe. He tried not to stare, but it was almost impossible.

The man spoke. "My sister and I are looking for a present for our little sister. We thought, perhaps, you could help us."

"Of course," said Otto, straightening his coat. "I will be happy to. Are you visiting?"

"No," said the woman. "Our family has moved here recently. From Garmisch-Partenkirchen."

She had the softest voice, like an angel, thought Otto, and smiled.

Fawn Island, The Pacific Northwest

Kiley smiled at the shop owner after he'd finished his story. "I take it she was the angel Otto saw in the snow globe."

He grinned. "So the story goes. Two Christmases later Otto had both a new wife and a new baby." He motioned to the lovely antique sitting on the counter. "That was passed down through Otto's family from generation to generation, always bringing hope when someone needed it most. At least that's what Mrs. Ackerman says."

"The woman you got it from," said Kiley and he nodded. "But why would she let it go?"

"She's Otto's last descendant, and she has no children. She felt it was time for it to pass on to fresh hands. But not necessarily to a collector." He gave a little shrug. "So she sent it off with a hope and a prayer that the snow globe will work a holiday miracle for someone new." He cocked an eyebrow. "Would you say you qualify?"

No boyfriend, no job? "I'd say I'm overqualified." Kiley looked at the little globe sitting on its ornate base. Costly as it was, she was sure it was underpriced. Even if it had gone for a small fortune at some fancy auction house it probably would have been underpriced. It symbolized hope, and how did you put a price tag on hope? She chewed her lip, trying to figure out how she could possibly afford it. Of course, she couldn't. But, darn, she needed it!

The shop owner smiled. "Tell you what. I'll take fifty percent off."

Fifty percent off—it was a sign. How could she refuse? She had just swallowed the last of her doubts and handed over her charge card when the bell over the shop door jingled. "We came to save you from yourself," said a familiar voice. Suz.

She turned to see her friends Suzanne Stowe and Allison Wright entering the shop. Suzanne was small; Allison was taller and about three sizes bigger. Both were blondes. A gust of wind whipped in with them, bringing the smell of Northwest rain into the stuffy little shop.

Suzanne looked at the assortment of china, knickknacks, and mysterious kitchen tools from another era, and wrinkled her perfect nose, hunching inside her North Face jacket like a turtle pulling into its shell. She didn't like the smell of anything old. Pottery Barn and Crate and Barrel were more her style.

But Allison looked eagerly around like a kid on a treasure hunt. She joined Kiley at the counter, holding out a disposable cup and sending the aroma of coffee dancing around Kiley's nose. "For energy."

"I don't need a latte, really," insisted Kiley, feeling guilty that her friends were picking up the tab for all her treats.

"Sure you do," said Suzanne. She started a fast stroll down an aisle, a petite vision in Northwest casual, her jeans showing off perfect thighs, her blond ponytail swinging.

Allison pointed to the bubble-wrapped snow globe the shop owner was slipping into a bag. "Did you get something cool?"

Kiley could feel a blush race across her face. She'd almost backed out of this weekend with her two best friends, claiming to be too broke, and now here she was spending a fortune on something her common sense insisted she didn't need. "He gave me a deal," she explained.

Allison smiled at her. "It's okay, Kiles. After all you've been through you deserve a treat."

"It's more than a treat," insisted Kiley. It was . . . well, she wasn't sure. She only knew it was somehow meant for her.

Suzanne had finished her quick tour of the store and now she joined them at the counter. "I'm hungry. Anybody ready for lunch?"

Allison nodded and followed Suzanne to the door and Kiley thanked the shop owner and hurried after them.

"I can't believe you found something in that musty old place," said Suzanne as they started for their favorite restaurant.

"Wait till you see it," said Kiley.

"Okay, I'm dying of curiosity," said Allison after they were seated inside the Chanterelle and had ordered the soup of the day and some of the restaurant's herbed bread. "Let's see your bargain."

Kiley pulled out her purchase and told them its legend.

The waiter arrived with a basket of warm bread. Allison started to reach for it, but then, true to her resolve to not get carried away with the carbs, picked up the snow globe instead and jiggled it. All three women watched the tiny snowflakes drift around the little angel. "It is lovely," Allison murmured as she set it on the table.

"But what a bunch of bull," Suzanne said. Her cell phone rang and she reached into her purse.

Allison frowned. "I thought you turned that off."

"I had to make a call," Suzanne said defensively. Suzanne always had to make a call. If not to check in on her five-year-old daughter, Bryn, then to see how things were going with her latest real estate deal.

Like Kiley, Suzanne had come close to canceling on their

weekend. Money wasn't a problem for her, but her busy schedule was the sworn enemy of girlfriend time. It happened a lot lately and Allison had finally put her foot down, insisting they all go so they could recharge and reconnect.

Allison's frown grew deeper when she realized Suzanne was talking to the agent she partnered with at Dreamscape Realty.

Getting the message, Suzanne finished her business quickly. "There. Done," she announced.

"Prove it and turn off your cell," Allison commanded.

Suzanne practically paled. "I can't. What if there's an emergency?"

"At home? Guy can handle it," Allison said.

"I know. I meant at work."

"That's why you have Julie," Kiley reminded her.

Suz turned off her phone with a frown.

Allison smiled, happy to have won the battle. "We need this, and it's not a getaway if you're not getting away."

"Fine," said Suzanne, "but tonight I'm checking my messages." She picked up Kiley's snow globe and examined it. "This is kind of cool," she admitted.

"And who knows," added Allison, "maybe it will bring something great into your life this holiday season."

Kiley sighed. "I almost wish I could climb into it and stay. At least until after Thanksgiving." Then she wouldn't have to face her unfaithful boyfriend and her sister the traitor.

"I'd join you in a heartbeat," Allison said with a sigh. "I'd put my grandma in there, too. Gosh, I hate to face the holidays without her."

"You'll get through them," Suzanne assured her.

Kiley took the snow globe back and studied it. "What is it about these things that makes you wish you could live in one?"

"Escape," said Suzanne. The waiter set steaming bowls of mushroom soup in front of them and she inhaled deeply and smiled. "Everyone has times when they don't like their life."

"Like every time I have to hang out with my family," Allison said with a shake of her head.

Kiley could understand Allison wanting to escape. She had seen just enough of her friend's family to know she didn't want to see any more. Well, except for Allison's grandma. But Suz? That seemed hard to believe.

"Maybe that's why we love things like this," Allison mused. "They give us hope that our lives can be different, better."

The little snow globe would have to work pretty hard to get Kiley to that point. But, hey, she still believed in miracles.

TWO

It would be a miracle if she didn't throttle her younger sister, Kiley decided, as she got ready to drive over to her parents' house on Thanksgiving Day. Well, she'd just avoid the traitor. And the two-timer. She had plenty of other people to focus on: Mom and Dad, her older brother, Corey, and his wife, Tara, and their four-year-old twins, Beau and Christopher, and her aunt and uncle and the cousins. She would simply pretend her sister didn't exist.

It was difficult to pretend Gwinnie didn't exist, though, when she did such a good job of grabbing the spotlight. Today she would show up in tight jeans and a sweater with a low V-neck, and she'd wear her long fake-blond hair down so she could flip it back over her shoulder on a regular basis. Kiley could do the hair flip thing, too. Only her hair wasn't blond so obviously it didn't have the same effect. Why hadn't Jeremy told her he preferred blondes? Or maybe it was that he preferred former cheerleaders to runners. Or maybe he didn't know what he wanted besides showing up and ruining her Thanksgiving.

"If you need to skip this year, everyone will understand," Mom had said. She'd phoned Kiley when Gwinnie arrived with Jeremy in tow. "I'm so sorry," Mom had added. "I never dreamed your sister would be so thoughtless. And Jeremy, I don't even know what to do with him."

Kiley could think of a couple of things, but none were anything a girl should say to her mother. "I'm coming," she'd said between gritted teeth. Those two had ruined her Halloween. She wasn't going to let them ruin her Thanksgiving, too.

She teamed her hottest sweater (red—men loved red, right?) with black pants and slipped into her sexy black heels. That would show him what he lost. She also packed her tennis shoes and sweats because she would be expected to participate in the annual post-dinner football game at the East Queen Anne playground: touch football, two hands anywhere—a rule the guys had established once they all started getting girlfriends.

The thought of seeing Jeremy putting his hands all over Gwinnie made Kiley's stomach clench. That won't happen, she told herself. Gwinnie had been opting out on football since two Thanksgivings ago when she fell and wrenched her knee. She had milked that injury for all it was worth, letting the cousins carry her to the car, taking over Dad's easy chair in the living room with an ice pack and occasionally whimpering to make sure she got waited on hand and foot the rest of the day. Not that Kiley had complained. She'd felt bad for Gwinnie and had done her share of the waiting. After all, she loved her little sister. Or had. Now she wasn't so sure.

Of course you love her, she reminded herself, as she stood in front of the bedroom mirror for one last check. Okay, so Kiley had hazel eyes, not blue. And so her nose was a little long. She still wasn't an arf-arf, and she was a good person. She was not the problem. Neither was Gwinnie. It was Jeremy. He was the one who had done the dumping. He was the one who had chased after someone else.

But Gwinnie didn't have to let him catch her.

That was love for you. It trampled everything in its path, even sisters.

She looked to where the snow globe sat on her dresser. Nothing had changed inside it. The little angel still stood duty in the Alpine village, guarding the toyshop.

Kiley shook her head in disgust. *What had you expected to see in there, Jeremy on bended knee in front of you, begging you to take him back?*

That was not going to happen. He wouldn't beg and she wouldn't take him back even if he did. She ran a finger over the snow globe. "I know I'm not widowed like Otto, but I could sure use some help." She picked it up and gave it a shake. Snow swirled and then settled on the cobblestone street. The scene remained the same.

She returned it to the dresser with a sigh. If this were a movie the angel would pop out of its glass cage and wrap her safely in those gold-tipped wings or she would get pulled right into that idyllic scene and meet Prince Charming. But she was no Disney princess and she had Thanksgiving dinner to get to.

She climbed into her Honda and drove under a grumpy gray Seattle sky from her two-bedroom condo on Kinnear to her parents' brick Tudor on the other side of Queen Anne Hill. Halfway there Amanda Overmyer came on the radio, belting "I Hate Myself for Loving You," and Kiley shut her off with a growl.

She arrived to find an army of vehicles already lined up along the parking strip and across the street, everything from SUVs to a Prius, telling her that she was the last one to arrive.

She winced at the sight of Jeremy's secondhand BMW. He had probably been the first one through the door. Dad would have let him in with a grunt and then left it to Gwinnie to entertain him. Dad's observation on the situation: "The dumb kid doesn't know what he wants."

Mom, ever the peacemaker, would be nice to him. After all, she had to. He was likely still going to be her son-in-law. Her take on the situation? "Obviously, he wasn't the right one for you, sweetie, and that means someone better is right around the corner. Meanwhile, keep the ring." Kiley had, and she'd sold it on eBay. So at least she wouldn't have to worry about condo payments for a couple of months. Not much of a silver lining, but it was something. As for the "someone better" waiting around the corner, sometimes Kiley wondered how far away that corner was or if it was even in the same city.

She took a deep breath. Then she gathered her purse, her football clothes, and the grocery bag with the punch makings she'd brought, and left the safe cocoon of her car.

Although her parents had done some renovating after they bought the house in the eighties, they had kept intact its best features—the old stone fireplace, the hardwood floors, and the arched doorways. Mom wasn't much of a gardener, but she'd fallen in love with the little rose garden in the corner of the front yard and had done her best to keep the roses healthy. Another one of the things she'd insisted on keeping was the enormous monkey tree that grew near the front walk. "It has character," she maintained. That it did—an evil character. The thing was the size of a small skyscraper and needed to be trimmed. Its prickly branches reached for Kiley as she made her way up the walk.

The front door was unlocked, and as Kiley let herself in the aroma of roasting turkey and the sound of a football game on TV greeted her along with raucous male laughter punctuated by the high-pitched squeals of a child. She rounded the front hall corner in time to see her burly cousin Mark tossing her four-year-old-nephew Beau into the air. The child's brown curls bounced and he let out a fresh shriek. If Beau was having this much fun it meant his twin Christopher couldn't be far behind. Sure enough, Beau's mirror image charged into the living room from the other direction and latched onto Mark's legs. Her other cousin, Zach, who was equally muscled, pried him off and sent him in the air, too. Meanwhile, Pansy, her parents' toy poodle, added to the confusion by yapping at them all.

Next to her Uncle Al, her brother Corey sprawled on the couch, a freckle-faced giant, grinning complacently while his cousins tossed the boys around like nerf footballs. Dad was being one with his easy chair, happily tolerating the abuse of his only grandchildren. And there, on a chair in the other corner of the room, sat Jeremy, resplendent in holiday casual clothes and acting as if he still belonged here. Which he did. Which made her stomach clench again.

Kiley was wondering if she was going to cry when Corey happened to glance her way and see her standing in the doorway. "Hey Road Runner," he called. "About time you got here."

Road Runner. It had been her nickname since she took up track in high school.

"Hi, Super Jock," she shot back. Her brother was now a football coach at a small high school in eastern Washington and she didn't get to see him nearly as often as she'd have liked. He still looked fit enough to get on the field and mow down a quarterback. When he first heard about the breakup he'd called and offered to crush Jeremy for her, adding, "Gwinnie can always find another idiot."

The sight of her made the idiot squirm in his seat. A bigger woman would have felt bad for him, Kiley supposed.

"Hey, Kiles," said Mark. He set Beau down and came to scoop her up in a bear hug. "You're lookin' good."

She couldn't resist stealing a glance in Jeremy's direction. Did he think she was looking good? Did he wonder what the heck he'd been thinking when he dumped her?

He was licking his lips, running a finger along the collar of his Polo shirt as if his neck was being squeezed by an invisible necktie. He nodded in her direction and gave her an uncertain smile. She ignored it, hugging each of her little nephews, who had started clamoring for her attention. She kissed her father on the top of his head, waved at her other cousin and her uncle, and then left to deliver the punch makings to the kitchen. There. That had been easy.

Except Jeremy was only one half of the traitor team. Gwinnie still waited in the kitchen.

Kiley took a deep breath. *You can do this.* She forced herself to walk through the dining room to the kitchen and run the next gauntlet. Grandma was still in charge of the gravy and stood at the stainless-steel stove, wearing her favorite slacks with the elastic waistband and a floral blouse, wiping her brow and stirring while Mom checked on her famous pumpkin rolls.

At Mom's state-of-the-art refrigerator, Kiley's sister-in-law, Tara, six months pregnant, paused in the middle of handing a huge bowl of fruit salad to Aunt Marion, gaping at Kiley as if uncertain where to place her family loyalties.

And, speaking of loyalties, there at the sink, whipping cream so she would have an excuse to continually dip her fingers in the bowl and sample, stood Gwinnie, dressed in jeans and the low-cut sweater Kiley had predicted she'd be wearing. Blond, blue-eyed, and beautiful—every man's dream.

Kiley narrowed her eyes and marched into the kitchen with murder in her heart.

THREE

The only thing that saved Gwinnie from annihilation was Mom looking up from the oven and beaming lovingly at Kiley, saying, "Hello, sweetie." She took out the baking sheet with the rolls and then hurried forward to kiss Kiley, cutting off access to Gwinnie the traitor. Mom was obviously psychic and knew what Kiley was contemplating.

Or maybe she's simply glad to see you, Kiley told herself, and hugged her mother. "Sorry I'm late."

"It's okay." Mom planted a kiss on her cheek. "We're just glad you're here."

Kiley wished she could say the same thing. Normally, the smell of roasting turkey set her mouth watering with anticipation, and the sight of her family filled her with joy. Today the smells and sights of the holiday were wasted on her.

She forced a smile and gave her sister-in-law a wave and a hi. Poor Tara. She was trying, like Switzerland, to remain neutral.

"You're just in time to help get food on the table," said Kiley's aunt, stopping to kiss her before proceeding on to the dining room with the fruit salad.

Kiley went to where Grandma stood at the stove and kissed her wrinkled cheek. Grandma studied her carefully. "How are you?"

What a loaded question! "I'm fine," she told both Grandma and herself. She'd be even finer once this day was over.

"Hi, Kiles," said a deliberately perky voice.

She turned with a frown to see Gwinnie, wearing a false smile, determined to act as if nothing was wrong.

A montage of scenes raced through Kiley's mind: she and Gwinnie wrapping a loop of elastic around chair legs and playing Chinese jump rope; Gwinnie asking Kiley to teach her how to make gum wrapper braids, and then hair braids; the two of them sprawled on the couch watching a late-night horror movie. The memories weren't enough to heal the hurt. In fact, they only inspired her to contemplate snatching the electric mixer and tangling its beaters in Gwinnie's hair.

"Hi, Gwinnie." She managed to get the words out, but she just couldn't add any warmth to them.

Gwinnie frowned and returned her attention to the whipping cream.

Kiley sighed inwardly and set her bag of goodies on the table next to where the punch bowl sat waiting. "I guess I'd better make this punch and take it out to the dining room," she muttered and got to work.

The kitchen went back to its busy buzz with the women putting finishing touches on the many dishes bound for the table and talk centered on the tasks at hand—"Do we have another serving spoon somewhere?" . . . "I think the gravy's ready." . . . "Gwinnie, stop whipping that cream before you turn it to butter."

This last comment came from Grandma, who was looking at her granddaughter with irritation.

Once upon a time—like last year, even—Gwinnie would have offered a beater to Kiley to lick. Today, she simply removed the beaters and laid them in the sink, then retreated to the fridge to put away the whipping cream for later when the pumpkin pie made its appearance.

Fine. Kiley didn't want to lick the beater anyway. She took the bowl of baby peas her mother handed her along with the mashed potatoes and went to the dining room.

"While you're at it, tell the men we're ready to eat," said Mom.

It didn't take more than one announcement to bring the men to the table. "This looks great," said Kiley's father, beaming with satisfaction at the feast laid before them, the fine china and crystal, and the cornucopia centerpiece. "You've outdone yourself this year, love," he told Mom as everyone settled in.

He said the same thing every year. And, as she did every year, Mom rolled her eyes and waved away the compliment. "Hurry up and say grace, John, before the natives get restless."

Dad complied, and the second he was finished the guys were all reaching for food. For the next few minutes, everyone concentrated on filling his or her plate and the conversational landscape was sparse.

Slowly, the time-honored topics surfaced. Which teams were going to the Super Bowl? How Grandpa would have loved to see this growing gang at the table, and, speaking of growing, had Tara and Corey settled on a name for the baby yet? Say, was this a new recipe for candied yams?

"Oh, I just haven't made it in a while," said Mom.

"Was it in the recipe book you gave me when we got married?" asked Tara.

"I think so," said Mom. "If not, let me know and I'll e-mail it to you."

"I want it, too," put in Gwinnie.

"Don't worry. You'll get it, along with all the other family recipes, when you get married," Mom said absently, and then looked like she wished she could swallow her tongue.

An awkward silence landed on the table and camped there. Eyes shot this way and that, everywhere but Kiley's direction. She was aware of Gwinnie regarding her nervously and Jeremy once again trying to loosen that invisible tie, and suddenly felt a lump in her throat the size of a golf ball, but she gamely scooped up a forkful of mashed potatoes and oh-so-calmly inserted them in her mouth.

Grandma came to the rescue. "Recipes might make a nice Christmas present for both our girls. I've been thinking it's time I parted with the one for my Christmas cake."

"I'd love to have that," Tara said eagerly, obviously happy to help steer the conversation in a safer direction.

Kiley kept her eyes on her mashed potatoes.

After dinner the men cleared the table and vanished into the kitchen to wash dishes, while the women lingered over their coffee. Kiley wished she didn't have to linger. Once the kitchen was clean the gang would be off to work up an appetite for pie by playing football. She had no appetite, for either pie or football. How soon till she could leave?

Wait a minute, she thought. *Why should you be the one to leave? The ones to go should be Gwinnie and Jeremy. They're the problem, not you.* She looked across the table to see Gwinnie gnawing her lower lip and watching her, hoping for absolution.

She turned her head.

A few moments later, Corey was leading the pack from the kitchen. He clapped his hands together and rubbed them eagerly. "Okay, who's ready to get their ass kicked?"

"By who?" retorted Zach, who was now right behind his cousin.

Corey loomed over him. "By me, dude." He cocked his head, motioning for Kiley to follow. "Come on, Road Runner. You're on my team."

Now Kiley could see Jeremy smiling at Gwinnie. "Come on, Gwin," he said.

She shot a look in Kiley's direction. "I don't want to."

"Oh, no," said Zach, hauling her up. "Everybody plays, even sissy girls."

"I want to play," piped Beau.

"Another couple of years, bud," his father said, rumpling his hair.

"But I want to play, too," he whined.

"Me, too," put in his twin.

"Aw, let 'em," said Zach. "Like you said, everybody plays."

"Okay, then. But don't trample 'em," Corey added, pointing a warning finger at Zach.

Tara had come out in time to hear the tail end of the discussion and quickly vetoed her husband's decision. "Some games are for grown-ups and bigger boys. When you're a little bigger you can go," she told the boys firmly. "Anyway, Grandpa and Uncle Al need you two to stay here and play with them so they won't get bored."

"We're going to play some Wii bowling," added Dad, and that was all it took to change the twins' minds about football.

"Maybe I'll stay and play, too," said Kiley. Then she wouldn't have to watch Jeremy stealing kisses and hugging Gwinnie, like he used to do with her.

"Oh, no," said Corey, pulling her away from the table. "You're coming, too. Tara can't play this year, Dad's back is trashed, and Uncle Al's knee hurts. If you don't come we won't have enough people."

It was useless to protest. Kiley went to change. Unlike Gwinnie, who made a production out of everything, it didn't take her long. In comfortable sweats and with her hair caught up in a big bush of a sloppy bun, she felt more like herself. But she didn't look like much, especially when she compared herself to her sister, whose outfit was tight and pink and made her look like a cupcake. Jeremy had obviously done plenty of comparing himself, Kiley thought miserably as Corey loaded her into his car.

The cousins piled into the backseat, leaving Gwinnie and Jeremy to follow in Jeremy's car.

"Okay, what was that stunt about?" Corey demanded as soon as the door was shut.

She tried to play dumb. "What?"

"Hiding at home with Mom and Dad won't help you get past this," he continued.

"Yeah," put in Mark. "Anyway, if you ask me you had a lucky escape."

Some lucky escape. She got out with a broken heart.

"Really," added Zach in disgust. "The guy is a doof."

She turned in her seat to look at him. "What do you mean, he's a doof?"

Zach shrugged. "He just is, Kile. You can do better."

"Well, if he's such a doof why didn't any of you say something when we were first dating?"

"Like you'd have wanted to hear?" retorted Corey.

"Anyway," Mark added with a shrug, "he didn't seem like a total doof back then. But now that he's dumped you and taken up with Gwinnie . . ." Mark didn't finish the sentence, just shook his head.

"He runs like a duck," said Zach.

"Wears a Polo shirt to play football," Corey added with a snort.

He and the cousins were all in old jeans and ripped T-shirts, which they filled out with well-built pecs and abs. Compared to them Jeremy looked . . . small. And inferior.

Except he wasn't. He was sweet and thoughtful and loved to go to movies. Okay, so he'd never had any desire to run with her. They still had lots of fun together. At least they used to.

"Look, Road Runner," said Corey. "I know this is hard, but

you've got to believe us when we tell you that losing this clown is really a good thing. He'd have just turned out to be a starter husband for you. He wouldn't have been enough to keep you happy all your life."

"Hell, he won't even be enough for Gwinnie," cracked Zach.

"That'll never last," Mark agreed. "This guy doesn't know what he's doing. By next Thanksgiving he'll be history."

What were they saying? "You think he'll dump Gwinnie?"

"Bank on it," said Corey with a sad shake of the head.

"If she doesn't dump him first," said Zach. "So this year we may as well have some fun," he added with an evil grin that didn't bode well for Jeremy.

Even though she was still mad at her sister, Kiley felt a moment of concern. The men in her family didn't always stay in touch with their feminine sides and if they decided to punish Jeremy it would be sure to upset Gwinnie.

"You guys . . ." she began.

"Don't worry," Corey said easily, cutting off her protest. "We won't hurt him. Much."

Sure enough. As soon as they got to the field and started playing Jeremy became a tackling dummy. Kiley winced each time he got shoved and pelted with the football. "Sorry, man," said Zach with a smirk, after a bruising that made Kiley wince.

Finally, when Corey took Jeremy down, landing on top of him, a red-faced Gwinnie accused, "You're not supposed to tackle. You're *trying* to hurt him!"

"That was an accident," protested Mark. "Corey tripped."

Gwinnie burst into tears. "You're all being mean."

Jeremy limped over to her and put an arm around her shoulder. "It's okay, Gwin. I'm fine."

"No, it's not." She glared at the others, hands on hips. "You guys don't have any right to treat Jeremy like this."

"Oh, yeah?" retorted Mark. "Well, maybe you didn't have any right to treat Kiley the way you treated her."

The tears were streaming down Gwinnie's perfect face now. "You don't understand. We didn't plan on falling in love. We didn't mean to hurt anyone."

"You did, Gwin," Corey said quietly. "And you never thought about how hard it might be for Kiley today."

"I did so! And it's been hard for me, too." Gwinnie buried her face in her hands and began to cry in earnest.

Watching her, Kiley felt heartsick. What a mess. And maybe some of it was her fault. She should have hugged her sister when she first arrived, been friendly to Jeremy, acted like she didn't care. Then everyone would have been happy and no one would be fighting.

"It's okay," she said, and hugged Gwinnnie.

Gwinnie, ever the drama queen, threw her arms around Kiley and upped the tear production. "Please don't hate me, Kiles. I love him. I can't help it."

"Oh gawd, I'm gonna puke," drawled Zach.

"You are such a spoiled brat," Corey told Gwinnie in disgust and Jeremy, who should have jumped in to defend her, stood there with a spine like a cooked noodle.

He could have said, *Don't blame Gwinnie. This is all my fault. I'm sorry I've screwed up your Thanksgiving and your family.* Why wasn't he saying something? Maybe he didn't want Gwinnie to be upset any further. Or maybe he *was* a doof. Or maybe Kiley was just bitter.

"This is lame," said Mark. "We may as well go back and eat pie."

And so, for the first time ever, the game ended on a sour note.

Back at the house, Dad and Uncle Al were playing Wii with the twins while Pansy yapped encouragement. The women were still parked at the dining room table, visiting. Corey and the cousins went to the punch bowl to rehydrate, Jeremy went to sponge off his dirty pants, and Gwinnie plopped onto the couch to pout.

Kiley decided she'd had enough fun for one day. She gave her mother a kiss on the cheek and said, "I'm going to take off."

"Already?" protested her aunt.

"I think I'm getting a migraine," she lied. Her mother studied her with concern and she felt her face warming under the scrutiny.

Thankfully, Mom didn't ask her what was wrong. Instead, she rose and led Kiley to the kitchen, saying, "Well, then, let's get you some pumpkin pie to take home." Once it was just the two of them, Mom said, "I'm sorry this day has been so hard for you, sweetie, but I'm proud of you for being brave enough to come."

She hugged Kiley, and that broke the dam. "How am I going to get over this, Mom?" cried Kiley, tears streaming down her cheeks. "I still want him. And I hate her. I know she's my sister, but I hate her."

"I know," Mom said softly, patting her shoulder. "Right now you do. But this ugly storm will blow over, I promise."

"When?" Kiley cried. "When will I see a rainbow? It's not that I don't want Gwinnie to be happy. But why does she have to buy her happiness with my misery? My God, Mom, it's been one thing after another this year. I wish I could catch even a glimpse of happiness."

Her mother took Kiley's tear-stained face in her hands and gave her the kind of bracing look only mothers can master. "I know you've had a double whammy, but you are a strong young woman, and a good one, and goodness never goes unrewarded." With those words of wisdom and a ton of leftovers, her mother escorted her safely to the front door.

Kiley drove away with a sore heart, the image of Jeremy sitting on the couch next to a pouting Gwinnie and looking miserable imprinted on her brain. *Good. Misery loves company.*

"You had a lucky escape," she told herself for what felt like the millionth time. A man who could swear undying love to one woman and then dump her in a heartbeat for her sister wasn't a keeper. She should feel sorry for Gwinnie. And she would, if she ever got past feeling sorry for herself.

Back home she settled in with her cat, Furina, to watch a DVD and gorge on pumpkin pie. But even though the movie was a holiday favorite it couldn't hold her attention, and the pie tasted like ashes.

She finally gave up on both, took a shower, and went to bed.

Sleep wasn't kind to her. Instead of letting Kiley sink into dark oblivion, it tortured her. She dreamed she stood in a church festooned with flowers and full of people as Gwinnie's brides-maid, and instead of a gown, she wore a clown suit. On the other side of her sister stood Jeremy, resplendent in a ringmaster's red tuxedo and a black top hat. He leaned across Gwinnie and told Kiley, "I never wanted you."

All the wedding guests started laughing, and chanting, "He never wanted you."

"He did!" Kiley insisted, and Gwinnie reached over and grabbed her big, red clown nose, making it honk.

Her eyes popped open and she sat up with a gasp, scaring Furina off the bed. She let out a calming breath and pushed her hair out of her eyes. *Get a grip.* She scolded herself. *It was just a dream. Just a stupid, pie-induced dream.* She looked at her bedside clock. Three A.M. Good grief.

Time for a bathroom break. Then she'd go back to sleep, continue the dream, and give her sister a big kick in the butt with her clown shoe.

The little snow globe seemed to call to her as she passed her dresser. "You were a waste of money," she told it.

Waste of money or not, she couldn't resist the urge to jiggle it. *Wait a minute. What was going on here?*

FOUR

Kiley blinked in disbelief. The scene in the snow globe had changed. She still saw a toyshop, but this one appeared to be in Seattle, in what looked like the Pike Place Market. A huge Christmas tree decorated with kites and dolls, and stuffed animals adorned this new toyshop window. And where was the angel? Maybe off having dinner at Ivar's.

Her eyes were playing tricks on her, that was it. She shook the globe again, stirring up a fresh snowfall, and watched the same toyshop with the toy-laden tree in the window emerge as the storm subsided. What did it mean?

Once back in bed, she snuggled under the covers and thought about the story the antique shop owner had told her about the snow globe's history. What was it trying to tell her? She suspected she wouldn't know until she found that toyshop.

Come morning, she awoke to realize something was missing. It was the heaviness that had been pressing on her heart for the last few weeks. Gone just like that. Now, there was a miracle!

She threw off the covers and padded to the dresser to visit the snow globe. The modern toyshop she'd seen was gone and the angel and the Alpine village were back. She reached out for the snow globe, then pulled back her hand. Of course, she'd dreamed what she saw the night before. Why disappoint herself by picking it up? She'd only ruin her good mood.

She slipped into her reflective running gear and did her usual three-mile morning run. It was seven-thirty and normally Kinnear Street would be bustling with cars. Every day she saw the bus on its way downtown and other joggers out on the street. But the early-bird shoppers were already at the stores today and everyone else in the civilized world was either still off visiting relatives or sleeping in. All she had for company this nippy morning was the sound of her breathing accompanied by the rhythmic pounding of her feet. She cleared her mind of everything but the sensation of fresh morning air and the pumping of her heart. After a mile, however, her mind began to wake up, and soon two words danced in time with every footfall. *Why not?*

Of course, it was silly to shake the snow globe again looking for some fairy-tale adventure. She'd been in a dream state when she saw that vision. What was the point in looking for something that wasn't real? She might as well plan to wait up for Santa on Christmas Eve. But . . .

Why not?

As soon as she got back home, she abandoned her earlier resolve, and picked up the snow globe and jiggled it. Her breath caught when the snow settled. There it was again. Okay, she told herself, It's broad daylight and I'm wide awake so I'm not dreaming. But she could be going crazy.

There was only one way to find out. She showered and made a protein drink with a banana mixed in for good measure. Then she parked on the couch with her drink and her laptop and began an Internet search. If there was a toyshop at the Pike Place Market, she'd find it.

She was barely into her search when her cell phone rang.

"Are you at the mall with your family?" asked Allison.

"Noooo. Yesterday was enough for a while."

"Oh. How'd it go?"

"Well, it wasn't fun," Kiley said. "But you know what? I think I'm over the Jeremy flu."

"The fever broke, huh?"

"Yes, it did."

"I'm glad," said Allison. "He doesn't deserve you."

"That's pretty much what Corey and the cousins think. And you know what, I think they're right." Kiley couldn't help smiling when she remembered how they had enjoyed pummeling her ex. Sick puppy that she was, she rather enjoyed the memory of it now. "How was your Thanksgiving? Do I dare ask?"

"No big fights."

"That's an improvement over last year," said Kiley, staying positive. "How long did you last with the wicked stepmother and the crazies?"

"An hour and a half. And she's not wicked. She's just . . . clueless and self-absorbed."

It amounted to the same thing as far as Kiley was concerned.

"Anyway, that checks off family togetherness until Christmas," said Allison. "Speaking of Christmas, how about going to Northgate with me? I want to make a dent in my shopping list."

"Actually, I may be doing some shopping, but not at the mall."

"Online?" Allison guessed.

"No, closer to downtown. Actually, I'm on a quest."

"Yeah? For what?"

"Promise you won't laugh?"

"Why would I do that?"

"Because it's going to sound crazy." Actually, it was, but, crazy or not, she had to find that toyshop and see what it had for her.

"Well, now I'm dying to know, so you'd better tell me."

"I saw something in the snow globe."

"Oh, my gosh!" squeaked Allison. "What?"

Kiley told her about the mysterious toyshop. "I have no idea what it means, but I have to go find that shop."

"I'll help you," Allison said eagerly. "Hey, maybe Suz wants to come, too."

"Not Suz," Kiley said. "She'll think we're both nuts. Anyway, I'll lay you odds she's working on that holiday home tour today. Or showing a house."

"Or both," added Allison. "Okay. It'll be just us. I'll be over in a few."

Half an hour later Allison arrived, wearing jeans, boots, and a red parka that made her look a whole size bigger than she was.

"Is it that cold out?" asked Kiley. Winters were almost always mild in Seattle, and she had opted for something a little more stylish.

"It's getting there," said Allison. "And I hate being cold."

So did Kiley. Still, she was willing to pay for style with a few shivers, so she stuck with her leather jacket, the one she'd bought back when she had a job and money. But since the weatherman was predicting some unusual weather for the weekend she added gloves and a wool scarf.

It was drizzling by the time they left and Kiley's carefully straightened hair began to frizz with the moisture. Great, she thought. Soon she'd look like a forsythia bush.

Even though most people were either in the downtown department stores or the mall, Pike Place had its own loyal following. In the summer, Seattleites brought friends and relatives to the historic farmers market that overlooked Puget Sound and the stunning mountain range beyond. There they'd watch the fishmongers toss salmon back and forth, or have their pictures taken with Rachel the bronze pig. The rest of the year they came to dine in the restaurants, pick up something tasty from the bakeries, or purchase fresh vegetables from the main arcade, and many a hostess could be seen heading home from the Market on a Friday with a huge bouquet of fresh flowers. In addition, the sprawling place offered any number of quaint shops and stalls where shoppers could buy wares from local artisans. And somewhere in the lower regions affectionately referred to by regulars as "Down Under," would be a mysterious toyshop.

"So, you're sure it's here?" Allison asked as they wandered past a couple of middle-aged women.

"Pretty sure," Kiley said, pulling off her gloves. There was *a* toyshop listed on the Market's website. Whether or not it was *her* toyshop remained to be seen.

"Let's ask somebody," Allison decided, and ducked into a shop that sold Asian art and clothing.

Kiley followed her in, feeling mildly stupid. She could have asked when they first arrived. *I'm looking for this toyshop I saw in my magic snow globe.* Hmmm. Maybe not.

"Is there a toyshop down here?" Allison asked the shop-keeper.

The woman's expectant smile faded and she pointed farther down to the end of the building. "That way. Keep going. You'll see it."

Somehow, it seemed wrong to come in and ask a shopkeeper directions to a different store, especially when there were no potential customers browsing, so, ignoring the funky smell of incense, Kiley drifted over to a display of scarves under a sign that read SALE. BUY ONE, GET THE SECOND FIFTY PERCENT OFF.

The woman's smile had returned. "When you buy one you get the other half off," she said, in case there was any doubt as to the veracity of the sign.

Kiley fingered one, taking in the bold pattern and vivid colors. "Oooh, that's gorgeous," said Allison, now at her elbow.

"You like it? Good," said Kiley. "Try to act surprised when you open your present."

Allison frowned. "Actually, I was thinking maybe we shouldn't exchange presents this year. I'm broke."

Kiley narrowed her eyes. "No, you're not."

"I need to save money," Allison said.

"And I don't have any?" Kiley added, getting to the heart of the matter.

"I don't want you to buy me anything," Allison said earnestly. "You can't afford it."

That was so typical of Allison. She was always thinking of others. Between her clueless father and her self-absorbed stepmother it was a miracle she had turned out so well. If it hadn't been for her grandmother, Allison would probably have drifted off into Flake Land right along with the rest of her screwy family.

"Well, I'm going to get you something," Kiley insisted, "so it may as well be something you want."

"Second scarf is half price," chimed in the shop owner.

"I'll get one for you and one for Suz," Kiley decided. She started sorting through them. "Help me pick one out that she'll like."

Allison gave up with a sigh, and five minutes later they left the shop with Kiley carrying a bag and Allison frowning in disapproval. "I thought we were going on a quest," she said.

"We are. But we're Christmas shopping, too. At least I am. Even unemployed people have to celebrate the holidays, you know."

Allison shook her head. Then she stopped and grabbed Kiley's arm. "Is that it?"

Kiley stopped, too, and gaped. There was the tree in the window, decorated with kites and stuffed animals. FOREVER KIDS, read the store sign. "Yes," she said breathlessly.

A tall man dressed casually in jeans and a gray T-shirt with an old beat-up bomber jacket thrown over it appeared in the doorway.

"Oh. My. Gosh," said Allison. "You saw *him* in the snow globe? I wish I'd bought it."

Kiley's mouth went dry. "All I saw was the shop."

"Well, then, he's a bonus."

He sure was. Even in the dim light of the market's lower level it was easy to see that he was fantasy-beautiful. His brown Indiana Jones hat hid his eyes but it couldn't hide a gorgeous mouth and a strong, Superman jaw. He stood for a minute in the doorway, looking at his display window like a king surveying his kingdom. Then he took a key from his pocket and inserted it in the door.

"He's locking up!" cried Allison. "Oh, no."

"Wait!" called Kiley, and they both took off at a run.

FIVE

The man looked up in surprise, then watched with a curious smile as the women dashed up to him.

"You can't be closing already," Allison protested. "It's only ten-thirty."

He pointed to a little cardboard sign with a clock hanging on the door. BE BACK BY . . . , promised the sign, and the clock was set to eleven A.M. "I was just going to Starbucks to grab a coffee. But I'm happy to open back up right now," he added, smiling at Kiley.

What a great smile. Up close Kiley could see that he had brown eyes, and dark hair fringed over his ears. And he was much taller than Jeremy. She came up only to his shoulder. She put her hand to her wild hair and tried to smooth it down.

"Or we could have coffee with you and then come back and shop," Allison boldly suggested, and Kiley felt herself blushing. *Subtle. Very subtle.*

"You probably don't want company," Kiley quickly added,

overcorrecting for her friend's pushiness. "We can do some more shopping and come back."

He motioned for them to join him. "It's not every day two beautiful women come running up and ask to have coffee with me. I'm not letting this opportunity slip away."

Beautiful? Well, Allsion, thought Kiley. Still, his flattery was balm to her wounded ego and she found herself smiling.

They fell in step with him, introducing themselves as they went. In only a matter of minutes they had learned that his name was Craig Peters, that he was a Seattle boy born and raised, that he had worked in the corporate world long enough to decide it wasn't for him and that he considered himself a thirty-three-year-old kid. Hence the name of his shop: Forever Kids. "Just because you grow old doesn't mean you have to grow up," he said.

Did Mr. Perfect have Peter Pan syndrome? Kiley sure hoped not.

"So, isn't this a big shopping day at the mall? What brings you two here?" he asked. "Superior taste?"

No way was Kiley telling him she'd seen his shop in the snow globe. Even an oversized Peter Pan would have trouble swallowing something so preposterous. Instead, she said, "The Market's got character, and you can find some unusual gifts here."

"That you can," he agreed. "Were you coming to my shop to get something for your kids?"

Kiley saw him checking out her left hand, looking for a ring, and her heart shifted from its lackluster plodding of the past month to an excited skip. "I have nephews."

Allison's cell phone rang. She pulled it from her purse and

checked the screen. "It's Suz. I tell you what. You guys go ahead and get that coffee. I'll meet you back at the store." And then she slipped away, talking as she went, leaving Kiley alone with Craig.

He grinned. "Is your friend always that subtle?"

She could feel a fresh blush warming her cheeks. "Oh, yeah. It's her specialty."

At the coffee shop Craig held the door open for her, something Jeremy had never thought to do, something she had never thought to expect. The whoosh of the espresso machine as the barista steamed milk for lattes greeted her and the smell of brewing coffee embraced her. There was something so cozy about slipping into a coffee shop on a cold, misty day. She could almost forget the fact that she was unemployed. Looking at the handsome man next to her she could certainly forget the fact that she was no longer engaged.

"What'll you have?" he asked as they approached the counter.

The last thing she wanted was to come across as a coffee mooch. "Oh, you don't have to—"

"I know," he said with a smile. "I want to."

He seemed to really mean it so she requested a small eggnog latte and went to claim the last vacant table remaining in the shop, a high, small one meant for intimate conversation. She slipped onto one tall chair and occupied herself by gazing out the window. It was starting to rain in earnest and passersby were picking up their paces and putting up umbrellas. She was glad she was indoors and warm.

A couple of minutes later Craig joined her, sliding her cup in front of her.

"Thank you. I wish you hadn't."

"I had to," he said solemnly. "Now you'll feel so guilty you'll be sure to buy something at my shop."

She smiled and shook her head, then took a sip of her latte.

He removed his hat and dropped it on the table and she noticed that his hair was thinning on top. He'd probably be bald by the time he was forty but it wouldn't matter. He'd still have those warm brown eyes and that great smile.

"So, Kiley Gray, have you got a boyfriend?"

She pushed away her cup. "Not anymore. We broke up at Halloween."

Craig nodded and took a thoughtful sip of his coffee. "Scary timing. Was it serious?"

She nodded, surprised that she suddenly couldn't speak. She thought the fever had broken and she was over Jeremy. She *was* over Jeremy, but what she hadn't quite gotten over was the loss of that rosy future she had dreamed of.

"That sucks," Craig said.

"I guess it just wasn't meant to be," she said. That particular future was gone. But what was to stop her from creating a new, better future?

Craig didn't ask for details. Instead he saluted her with his cup. "Good attitude. There's plenty more fish in the sea."

And this particular one intrigued her. "Speaking of fish, why hasn't anyone caught you?" she asked, keeping her voice light.

"I'm slippery," he cracked. "Seriously, nothing's worked out. I've thought of trying one of those online dating services but I dunno. They seem so . . . planned. Where's the adventure?"

This man owned a toyshop. Of course, he'd want his search for Miss Right to be an adventure. Kiley couldn't help smiling.

He swallowed the last of his drink. "Why don't we go back to my shop? You can look around, and when you're done you can give me your phone number."

There was still no sign of Allison when they returned to the shop, but once inside Kiley forgot all about her friend as Craig gave her a tour of his kingdom. "Of course, we've got the video games. Gotta have that," he said, pointing to a corner packed with technology. "But when parents come in I usually steer them somewhere else."

Educational toys abounded, and puzzles, magic sets, marionettes, and old-fashioned tops. "I haven't seen one of these in years," Kiley said, running her finger along a fat, multicolored one.

"Those can keep a kid happy for hours," said Craig. "Heck, they keep me happy for hours," he added with a grin.

"My nephews are too old for that now."

"How old are they?"

"Five. They're twins."

"Ant farms are cool," he said.

"My sister-in-law would kill me."

"Sea monkeys? Every kid should have a chance to grow sea monkeys."

"Oh, I don't think so," she said diplomatically. Then she spotted the shelf with the kaleidoscopes. "I remember getting a kaleidoscope for Christmas when I was ten." She picked one up. It was made of wood and beautifully crafted. She put it to her eye and peered at a miniature stained-glass window. She turned the kaleidoscope, making the pattern shatter and reshape itself. "This is perfect."

"Well, okay," he said. "I was thinking kites, myself."

"Not for them. For me." She gave the end another twist and marveled at the new mosaic of color. One more turn, one more look. "Another time," she added, and reluctantly set it aside. "I'll take two kites. Not too expensive," she added.

"Got ya," he said, and led her to the window with the Christmas display and they spent several minutes discussing the merits of the kites hanging on the tree. Of course, he had more in another corner, set up over a tiny seaside scene, complete with sand and a beach umbrella. She finally decided on two octopus-shaped kites in two different colors.

"Good choice," he approved. "Those are just right for little kids. Anything else?"

Not until she got a job. "That will do it," said Kiley. But just because she was done didn't mean she couldn't look. And there was much to take in. Every corner of the shop had been arranged to look like a child's fantasy. Stuffed animals stalked each other in a jungle of plastic plants, bats and sports balls of every variety hung in a net over a mannequin dressed up in athletic shorts and a basketball jersey. Dolls had tea at a small table. How had he managed to fit so much merchandise in the small space and make it not feel crowded? "I could easily spend a fortune in here," she said, following him to the counter.

"Tell me about it. I have. So, do you work around here?"

"Farther uptown," said Kiley. "Or at least I used to."

"Used to?"

"I'm exploring new opportunities," Kiley said, trying to put a good spin on her present unemployed condition.

He gave a grunt and a sympathetic nod. "Been there, done that." He studied her a moment. "I don't suppose you design Web sites."

"I have." She remembered that she hadn't found one for his place. He was listed only under the market's Web site. "You don't have a site?"

"Haven't gotten around to it yet," he confessed. "I only bought the business last month." He shook his head. "The previous owner had pretty much run it into the ground. I got it for a song." He rang up her purchases and she handed over her trusty charge card. "I think I can make a go of it," he continued. "I'm already talking with some people about sponsoring a couple of kids' fairs in the spring. And I've got a Christmas ad campaign planned. But I need to get a Web site up ASAP." He handed back her charge card and she signed the receipt. "So, how about that phone number? I'm thinking we should have dinner and talk."

By the time Allison returned Kiley and Craig had a dinner date for that night and were already discussing ways he could promote the shop.

"Are you ready for lunch?" Allison asked.

Lunch? Kiley looked at her watch. It was almost twelve-thirty. Where had the time gone? "I guess so."

"Enjoy the rest of the your shopping," Craig said as they left.

"So, tell," Allison commanded as soon as the shop door shut behind them. "Is he as wonderful as he looks?"

"He could be," Kiley said. "Although I keep thinking this all seems too good to be true."

Allison frowned and shook her head. "That's what Suz says. But she's a cynic."

Kiley felt a sinking in her stomach. "You didn't tell her about what I saw in the snow globe, did you?"

Allison's guilty expression gave Kiley her answer.

"Great," said Kiley. "Just what I need, Suzanne telling me I'm hallucinating." Although maybe she was. Or maybe this was all a dream and she'd wake up any minute.

But that night, as she and Craig sat at a window table eating pasta in a cozy Italian restaurant on lower Queen Anne, she couldn't help hoping that if she *was* dreaming she wouldn't wake up.

It wasn't hard, listening to him talk, to see what a good heart he had. His mother had raised him and his brother single-handedly. He admired her greatly and helped her when he could, doing small repairs and keeping her lawn mowed. Most of his time was taken up with the toyshop. He'd left his corporate job to take a gamble on it and was hoping his savings would last until he turned the shop around. "I know I'm competing with the big chains and the Internet," he admitted, "but I think I can make a go of this. Plus, once I get the site up and running, I'll sell stuff on the Internet, too."

It was risky, but she couldn't help admiring his determination. "At least you only have yourself to worry about," she said.

"Pretty much."

"Pretty much? What does that mean?"

It meant that even though he had a business to launch he was still helping his little brother through college. Saint Peters.

"That's really sweet of you," said Kiley.

He shrugged. "Nah. I don't have to kick in that much. He's got some scholarship money and he's working part time."

"For you?" asked Kiley.

"Nope. He works weekends as a waiter. He can make more in tips than I can afford to pay him. Anyway, even though he thinks the shop is cool, it's not his dream. Well, will you look at that?" Craig said, pointing out the window. "I guess for once the weatherman was right. It hasn't snowed in Seattle on Thanksgiving weekend since I was a kid," he added in awe.

Kiley had noticed earlier that the temperature had dropped drastically. Still, in spite of the weatherman's predictions, she was surprised to see soft flakes drifting to the ground, dancing in and out of the beam of the streetlights. People hurried down the street, hunched inside their coats, their collars held tightly together. Here inside the restaurant it was warm and pleasant, a haven fragrant with the scent of Italian spices and simmering sauces.

They finished off their dinner with tiramisu and coffee, and then walked out into the frosty night. The snow was sticking now and a white carpet of flakes crunched beneath their feet as they walked. A winter wonderland, she thought.

Craig drove her home, letting his car radio serenade them. Then, at the door of her condo, he ran his fingers through her hair and kissed her good night. As her whole body warmed in his embrace she thought, If I could freeze one moment in a snow globe, I'd pick this one.

SIX

Saturday she half expected Craig to call, but he didn't. Well, he was trying to start a business. He'd probably call on Sunday. That night, before she went to bed, Kiley couldn't help visiting her magical snow globe one more time, and giving it a shake. As before, the snowstorm she started cleared, and again showed Craig's toyshop, but now there he was, too, standing in the doorway. It looked as if he was smiling at her. She gave the decoration a loving pat, and went to bed to dream.

Sunday was glorious. The snow fell all night, forcing busy city dwellers to slow down and enjoy life. Kiley was all for that. She dug out a pair of boots she hadn't used in years and donned her parka, hat, and gloves. Then she went out to put her mark on the pristine blanket that covered the sidewalk in front of her condo.

How different the city looked. The Space Needle reigned over a kingdom of white with snow-topped houses that made her think of the gingerbread artwork she loved to see on display at the downtown Sheraton Hotel every Christmas. Cement disappeared under a white carpet, and trees and shrubs sported lacy shawls. Laughter echoed to her on the crisp air.

She hadn't walked far before she saw a group of children building a snowman. They had given him a smile made of small rocks and popped two larger ones above it for eyes. Someone's mother had seen fit to donate a carrot for the cause, which they had used for a nose, and they'd found branches for his arms. But he was sadly lacking in wardrobe.

Inspired, Kiley stopped and offered them her knitted hat. Now her hair would go crazy, but oh, well.

"Wow, thanks!" said one of the girls. She took Kiley's offering and settled it on the snowman's head.

"That's a girl's hat," protested one of the older boys, eyeing the pink pompom at the tip of it in disgust.

"So?" retorted the girl.

"So boys don't wear hats like that," said the dissenter.

Neither did girls with any fashion sense, thought Kiley. It was a stocking cap that looked like the world's ugliest rainbow Popsicle. In short, it was the kind of hat that would have inspired the *What Not to Wear* duo to great heights of sarcasm. The only reason Kiley had donned the thing was because it was warm. Allison had made it for her a couple of Christmases ago, when her grandma was teaching her to knit combining different colored yarns, and Kiley had kept it out of a sense of girlfriend duty. Getting rid of it to support budding artists was, if Kiley did say so herself, brilliant.

Meanwhile, the battle over whether a wild colored chick hat

was acceptable snowman attire raged on. Finally the girl who had accepted it wadded a couple of handfuls of snow into a giant snowball.

Uh-oh, thought Kiley with a smile.

But instead of throwing it the girl pushed her lump of snow onto one side of the snowman's chest, saying, "Then we'll make it a girl."

The other children giggled and the dissenter pitched in to help give the snowman a sex change.

Oh, that all disagreements could so easily be solved, thought Kiley, and walked on. If that had been her and Corey and Gwinnie they'd have been pelting each other with snowballs until someone gave in—usually her or Gwinnie.

Gwinnie. Would she wind up at Jeremy's place today, curled up on his couch, watching movies? Would he make cocoa for her?

Did Kiley really care anymore? She smiled. No.

Her ears were starting to burn from the cold. Time to go home and pull a packet of hot cocoa mix out of the cupboard. She didn't need a man to make it for her.

Although she wouldn't object if a certain toyshop owner offered.

Back home she checked her cell for messages. Nothing from Craig Peters. He probably had to go shovel snow for his mother. Or something.

She did have one message, though. "Okay, what is going on?" Suzanne demanded. "Call me and fill me in. I'm snowed in so I'll be here."

To smother Kiley's good mood under an avalanche of

skepticism. She looked out her condo window at the wintry scene and sighed. It wouldn't last long. The fat, white drops lazily floating down would soon turn silver as temperatures rose, and rain would turn the pretty snow to slush. Then the fluke snowstorm would be gone as quickly as it had come and everything would be back to normal. Meanwhile, though, the view outside her window was storybook wonderful.

She decided she'd deal with Suzanne later. After she'd heard from Craig. He had all day.

She pulled out her favorite Starbucks mug and made herself some cocoa, then moved to her couch, where her cat Furina was already lounging. She and Jeremy had picked out this couch together—sage-colored microfiber, and on sale. It had been one of their first purchases for their new life.

Try not to think of it as losing a boyfriend but as gaining a couch, she'd told herself after they broke up. Now she told herself that maybe soon she'd have a new boyfriend to share her couch.

Furina let Kiley settle in with her cocoa before lazily stretching and relocating to Kiley's lap. Like all well-trained owners, Kiley knew what to do. She started petting the longhaired calico. "Yeah, I know. You just happened to be in the neighborhood and thought you'd drop in. Right?"

Furina purred as if to say, *Talk all you want but keep petting. My wish is your command.*

Furina had never warmed to Jeremy. She had mostly kept her distance and the few times he tried to pet her, she'd hissed at him.

"Maybe you were smarter than me," Kiley mused.

Furina purred on. *Yes, I am, but I love you anyway.*

"Well, it's a new day," Kiley murmured.

And, as if to prove it, her cell rang again.

Kiley's heartbeat picked up in anticipation and she snatched the phone from her coffee table. She looked at the screen and felt her spirits deflate. Suzanne again. "May as well get this over with, huh?" she said to Furina.

Suzanne barely gave her time to say hello. "Okay, what's this I hear about that snow globe helping you find the perfect man? Was Allison high on scented candles or something?"

"No," said Kiley with a frown.

"Look, I know you've had a rough month and—"

Kiley cut her off. "Friday wasn't just wishful thinking. It really happened and Allison is my eyewitness."

"She saw the toyshop in the snow globe?"

"No, but—"

"So, the only person who saw it was you? Maybe you just imagined you saw it," Suz suggested.

"If I only imagined I saw it, how did I find it?" demanded Kiley.

"I don't know," Suz admitted. "That part is weird."

"And what about the man I met?"

"Coincidence," Suzanne countered.

"Well, that's some coincidence," said Kiley.

"It's the only rational explanation."

When were miracles ever rational?

"Look, I just don't want you to rush into anything," Suzanne said, her voice softening. "After everything with Jeremy, well, you're vulnerable."

Jeremy. Her friends hadn't liked him any more than her cat. What vibes had they picked up on that she hadn't? Had she been so anxious to find someone that she'd dulled her senses? Was she doing the same thing now with Craig?

Kiley relocated Furina from her lap to the couch. Insulted, the cat jumped down and stalked off, asserting her independence. Kiley ignored her and went to the bedroom to where her snow globe occupied prime real estate on her dresser. The Alpine village was back once more. Suzanne was still talking, but Kiley tuned her out. Instead, she listened to the voice somewhere at the back of her mind that whispered, *Shake me.*

So she did. The little curtain of snow fell away and again she saw the Seattle toyshop and Craig Peters standing in the doorway. And . . . what was this? Someone new had joined him: a woman with long, curly brown hair who looked suspiciously like her. "Oh, my gosh," she gasped. "It's changed again."

"What?" Suz demanded. "What do you mean?"

"I'm in it. I'm in the snow globe with Craig."

"I don't like this," Suzanne said in a low voice. "I'm coming over."

"You don't drive in the snow," Kiley reminded her. *Thank God.*

"I just heard the weather report. It will be slush by afternoon. I'll be there."

"Goody," muttered Kiley as she ended the call. She wandered back out into the great room area and saw that Furina was now prowling the kitchen counter. "You know better," Kiley scolded, and lifted Her Majesty off it.

Offended yet again, Furina jumped from her arms and returned to the couch, curling up on the afghan Allison had made Kiley as a housewarming present. Of course, she would leave as much fur on the cream-colored blanket as possible. Kitty revenge.

Kiley had barely reheated her cocoa when the phone rang. This time—big surprise—it was Allison.

"I got tired of waiting for you to call. How was dinner?"

"Fabulous."

"And what about the snow globe? Did you see anything new?"

"I did." Happiness settled over Kiley like a cloak. She closed her eyes and savored the feeling. It was one she'd almost convinced herself she'd never have again. How wonderful it was to be wrong!

"What did you see?"

"Well, I saw the toyshop again. And Craig."

"And?" prompted Allison.

"And a woman."

"Was it you?"

"Yep."

"Oh, my God. That is sooo romantic. I wish I'd bought the thing."

"You already have a boyfriend," Kiley reminded her.

Allison gave a little grunt. "Lamar, God's gift to womankind. Let me tell you, I'm not sure how much longer I'm going to have him."

So, Lamar was in the doghouse again. It happened on a regular basis, but he always charmed his way back out. Sometimes Kiley wondered if Allison kept the studly Lamar simply because she didn't want to part with his mother and grandmother, who were more like a family to her than the dysfunctional one she was stuck with.

"Anyway, never mind about him," Allison said briskly. "Tell me more about Mr. Wonderful. What did you guys talk about at dinner?"

"Everything and anything. You know he grew up here in Seattle. Went to Ballard High. And he was on the track team."

"A runner," Allison crowed. "Perfect. Did he say he'd call you?"

"As a matter of fact, he did. I'm going to design a Web site for him, and I'll probably help him with his online store, too."

"I'm so glad for you, Kiles," said Allison. "And what an amazing way to find your perfect man. Except no one will ever believe it when they hear how you found him."

"Suzanne sure doesn't," Kiley said. She guessed she couldn't blame Suzanne. It did all sound pretty far-fetched. "She's coming over later to see for herself, thanks to a certain big mouth."

"I know, I know," said Allison. "I probably shouldn't have told her. But it's just so awesome. Maybe I'll have to come, too. I'm dying to see the snow globe in action."

"Sure. Why not," said Kiley, resigned to her fate. She'd nursed the hope of having company before the day was over. Only she'd envisioned someone with a lower voice and slightly different body parts. She looked out the window to see that the white flakes had already morphed into silver slivers. Seattle's famous rain was back and soon the snow would be nothing but a pleasant memory, a weather anomaly to be discussed around water coolers and on morning walks around Green Lake. He could still call, still come.

"I'll bring brownies," Allison offered. "I'm making a ton for Suz's holiday home tour."

Allison was a physical therapist by day, but in her off hours she channeled Julia Childs, and she picked up extra money catering Suzanne's events.

Kiley's taste buds suddenly took an active interest in the conversation. "Those mint ones?"

"Those would be the ones. I'll see you later."

All right. Chocolate mint brownies weren't on a par with spending the evening with Craig Peters, but she'd make do.

Suzanne was the first to arrive. "Thank God the snow is going away," she said as she blew into the condo in a mist of perfume and style. Her red scarf was cashmere, the coat was a black wool number from Nordstrom's—not from the Rack, where Kiley occasionally prowled for bargains. The boots were from Nordy's, too. Suzanne had bragged about getting them on sale, although even on sale they'd been too rich for Kiley's blood. But Suzanne settled for only the best. She once said she'd walk barefoot before she'd buy bargain chain-store shoes.

"I kind of hate to see it melt so quickly," Kiley said.

Suzanne frowned. "That's because you are currently unemployed and don't have to be anywhere." She pulled off the scarf, shaking her blond hair free, then hung her coat in the closet where Furina couldn't reach it.

"You're self-employed," Kiley reminded her. "You could take a day off."

Suzanne shook her head and looked regretful. "Not if I want to pay my mortgage."

She and Guy had bought and refurbished an old house on Magnolia. It had been about to go into foreclosure, and thanks to her real estate connections Suzanne had gotten it for a song. But the more she talked to the architect and interior designer the grander the song had gotten. Now she had a gorgeous house with refinished hardwood floors, crown molding, and expensive furniture that she enjoyed on the rare occasions she wasn't working. She also had huge payments, which gave her the perfect excuse to remain a workaholic.

"Anyway, I did take time off." She whipped out her digital camera from her purse and displayed the evidence. "See?"

Yes, sure enough. There she was, rosy-cheeked and beautiful in jeans and a white parka, black mittens on her hands, a black cashmere scarf around her neck and a matching black tam on her head. Next to her, holding her hand, her daughter, Bryn, looked like a miniature Suzanne, bundled into a pink snowsuit, her golden curls poking out from under a pink hat.

They stood beside a snowman wearing a very ugly scarf. Kiley recognized those colors. Obviously, when it came to figuring out how best to use Allison's early craftwork, great minds thought alike. The snowman's wardrobe didn't catch Kiley's eye as much as the expression on Bryn's face. She looked up at her mother as though Suzanne was the Madonna.

And Suzanne's expression? It was one Kiley recognized. It

said: *Okay. Snowman completed? Check. Now, let's get on to the next thing on the list—pronto.* And there was always a next thing on the list. Suzanne liked to live in the moment, the moment that belonged to the future. She was constantly looking ahead: to the next decorating project, the next listing, or the next sale, busy building an empire in which her home was the crown jewel. Kiley admired her friend's efficiency, but she sometimes worried that Suz didn't really appreciate how much she already had.

"So, let's see the snow globe," said Suz, cutting to the chase.

"How about a cup of tea first? Allison's coming over with chocolate mint brownies."

"Her Christmas ones?" Suzanne asked hopefully. Kiley nodded and she said, "Okay, I'll wait."

"What do you mean wait?"

"Well, I can't stay too long. I have to run over to the office and do a couple of things."

"You know, rest is not a four-letter word," said Kiley.

Suzanne made a face. "I'll rest in January, but right now I have a million things to do for the holiday home tour." She checked her watch, reminding Kiley of the White Rabbit in *Alice in Wonderland*.

"You don't have to stay, you know," Kiley said, miffed. "No one forced you to come over and check my grip on reality."

Suzanne's expression turned penitent and she let her hand fall to her side. "Sorry. But cut me some slack, okay? I wouldn't be here if I didn't care." She went to the couch and perched on one end. "Tea sounds great." As Kiley moved to the stove to heat water for brewing she saw Furina stalking toward Suzanne's lap. Suz held up a hand, stopping the cat in her tracks. "Don't even think about it."

Furina jumped off the couch and walked away, tail held high. Poor Furina. Suzanne had never allowed her within lap range after the night Furina yakked up a fur ball on the cream-colored sweater Suz had left laying on a chair.

The doorbell rang and then the door flew open. "I'm here," announced Allison. "Let the brownie binging begin."

That brought Suz off the couch.

Kiley started herbal tea steeping in her Fiestaware pot, then joined her two friends at the kitchen counter, where Allison had set down a small decorative Fitz and Floyd Christmas plate laden with brownies thickly topped with green frosting and sprinkles.

"Oh my gosh, I think I just gained two pounds from simply looking at those," said Suzanne, awe in her voice.

That was a joke. Suzanne managed her weight as efficiently as she did her calendar. Her body wouldn't dare harbor any fat.

Kiley never worried about her weight. Running burned up enough calories that she could splurge when she wanted. Which was just what she intended to do now. She picked one up and bit into it. Heaven.

Suzanne took a delicate nibble of one, then closed her eyes and savored. "Better than sex," she murmured.

"Nothing is better than sex," Allison informed her.

She merely shrugged. "This takes less energy." Both friends looked at her in disgust. "What?" she protested.

"If we have to explain, you're beyond help," Allison said sternly.

Any minute Suz was going to demand to check out the snow globe. "So, what does Bryn want from Santa this year?" asked Kiley, trying to postpone the inevitable.

Suz rolled her eyes. "A puppy."

"Aw, that's sweet," said Allison.

"Oh, yeah. It's especially sweet when the thing is whining to go out at two in the morning or when it pees on the carpet. No, thanks."

"You have hardwood," Kiley said dismissively.

"Excuse me? Are you forgetting my new Persian rug in the living room? Anyway, having a puppy would be just like having a baby and I don't have time," Suzanne added. She leaned on the counter and started in on another brownie.

"Even Martha Stewart has a dog," protested Allison.

"And a staff to train it," countered Suzanne. "Anyway, why are we talking about me? We're here to hear about Mr. Wonderful and gaze into the snow globe."

Allison took a brownie from the plate, looked at it longingly, and then returned it. "Has he called yet?"

Kiley picked it up, broke it in two, and handed Allison half. "No. But we only met Friday," she said as much to herself as to her friend. And talked for hours and shared a good-night kiss that had curled her toes. Why hadn't he called?

"But he's perfect," said Allison. She took a bite of the brownie then threw the rest in the garbage. "And the snow globe led her to him."

Suzanne took a quick sip of her tea, then said, "Okay, I want to see this for myself."

"Doubting Thomas," muttered Kiley, but she took them to her bedroom. Furina was now stretched out on her bed, happily getting little black cat hairs all over her comforter.

Suzanne walked to where the snow globe sat on the dresser. "It is beautiful, I'll say that. I have to admit, if I'd seen it before you I'd have bought it. It would have looked great on my mantel." She picked it up and handed it to Kiley. "It's show time. Let's see it do its stuff."

Kiley made a face at her and took it. There was the Alpine village and the toyshop and the angel. Her heart sped up. What if, all of a sudden, it decided not to work?

"Come on," urged Allison. "I'm dying to see."

Kiley took a deep breath and gave it a jiggle. The snow swirled. And then settled. And there it was: Craig's toyshop. He still stood in the doorway. And she was there, too, right next to him, smiling up at him. A thrill ran through her and she grinned.

"Do it again," suggested Allison. "Maybe it needs to, you know, get warmed up."

Kiley blinked. "What do you mean? Don't you see it? There's the toyshop, there's Craig, there's . . ."

Both her friends were exchanging worried looks.

Her heart sank. "You don't see it?"

SEVEN

An uncomfortable silence settled over the room. Kiley gave the snow globe another shake and all three women stared at it.

"Sorry, Kiles," said Suzanne. "I'm still not seeing it."

Kiley looked hopefully to Allison, who shook her head slowly and said, "Maybe you're the only one who can."

"Or you dreamed what you saw," said Suzanne. "Didn't you say it was the middle of the night?"

"I saw it this morning, too, the same thing that's there now," Kiley insisted. "And I'm not imagining it." She set the snow globe back on the dresser and left the room. "Maybe it doesn't show itself to skeptics."

"I'm not a skeptic," Allison protested, following her out.

Suzanne fell in line behind them. "Okay, maybe it is there and I'm blind. And maybe you've found the perfect man and your future will be great. I mean, I hope you have. I just don't want you to get hurt, that's all. So don't be mad at me."

Kiley sighed. How could she be mad at a friend who cared

enough to worry about her? Suzanne was looking at her, defensive, hopeful, sympathetic. "I wish I could be."

Suzanne smiled and hugged Kiley. "Keep me posted on what happens with Toy Boy. If that snow globe works I may have to borrow it and ask it to show me where the buyers for the house on Eleventh Avenue are."

Leave it to Suz to want to turn the snow globe into an Aladdin's lamp.

Their friendship restored to an even keel, Suzanne pulled her coat from the closet. "I've gotta go. Allison, I'll talk to you more next week about the food for the home tour," she added. Then she was gone.

Allison shook her head. "How did we ever wind up becoming friends with such an overachiever?"

"You're a bit of an overachiever yourself, you know. Working full time and catering on the side."

"Yeah, but the catering is fun," Allison said with a grin. "Sometimes, when I'm in the kitchen, I can almost feel my grandma there with me." It had been almost a year since her grandmother died, but Allison's eyes still glistened with tears.

"She'd be proud of you," said Kiley.

"I hope so," said Allison, and wiped at a corner of her eye.

Kiley helped herself to another brownie. "So, do you think I'm nuts?" she asked, careful not to look at her friend.

"Absolutely not," Allison said firmly. "Of course, I'm probably the wrong person to ask. I still put out cookies for Santa."

Kiley regarded her skeptically. "You don't."

"Of course, I do." She grinned. "Then on Christmas morning

I eat 'em. Seriously," she added, "I believe in miracles. After all, isn't that what this time of year is all about?" She hugged Kiley. "And I believe you. If you say you see the toyshop and Craig in that snow globe then you do. And that's that."

Allison's support should have been enough, but Kiley found herself doubting her own eyesight. After Allison left she settled on the couch with the snow globe and started a blizzard. Even before the snow finished falling she could see the Pike Place toyshop. She was not imagining this. Couldn't be. But how could she prove it?

Inspiration hit. She jumped off the couch and ran for her digital camera. Allison hadn't been looking carefully enough. Suzanne had been deliberately blind. The light had been bad. As with many live shows, something had gone wrong. But this time she'd capture that image and then Suzanne would have to believe her. Camera in hand, she shook the snow globe and then set it on the coffee table and snapped the picture. Ha!

Smiling, she looked at the camera screen. There was the snow globe, but the Pike Place Market toyshop was nowhere to be seen. Instead, the angel in its Alpine village seemed to mock her. Icy fingers of fear ran over her skin and she dropped the camera. She *was* hallucinating. "I *am* going crazy," she said to herself in shock.

But crazy people didn't find a shop, let alone a man, that was an exact match to what they had seen in a snow globe, did they?

Kiley suddenly remembered Otto Schwartz, its original owner. He probably thought he was crazy when he first saw his future wife inside that glass ball, but a miracle happened anyway.

Miracles had a way of happening when people needed them most. Kings were born in mangers; angels serenaded shepherds. Not everyone saw miracles when they happened, but that didn't make them any less real.

She erased the false picture from her camera's memory card and returned the snow globe to her dresser. Then she settled in with her new issue of *Runner's World,* keeping the phone handy. Craig would call. They'd be together. It was her turn for a holiday miracle.

She got three more calls that night. One from Mom, asking how she was doing, another from Gwinnie, calling to reassure herself that Kiley hadn't yet disowned her, and another from a telemarketer. But nothing from Craig Peters. To distract herself from her disappointment and the possibility that she might be going insane, she watched her favorite TV shows until, finally, there was nothing left to do but to go to bed and feel let down.

She avoided even looking at the snow globe as she turned off the bathroom light and padded to her sleigh bed (the second purchase she'd made with Jeremy for their new life together).

Craig would call. Tomorrow.

Kiley began her next day with a morning run, splashing through puddles, enjoying air still fresh from the weekend's snowfall, breathing in, breathing out, welcoming the endorphins racing through her body as she jogged her way along the sidewalk. She returned home feeling energized. Until she checked her cell and found she had no messages.

He'll call, she told herself. Meanwhile, you have things to do. And to prove it, she spent the rest of the morning on the Internet, catching up on her social networking, searching job sites and sending off e-mails to let friends and former coworkers know that her services were now available if anyone needed a Web site designed or a mailing list managed or . . . anything. Just a couple of clients would keep her boat afloat until she found full-time employment again.

Having done all she could on the job front, she put on her favorite Carrie Underwood CD and went into a cleaning fever, singing along with "Before He Cheats" at the top of her lungs. Okay, all better now, she told herself. So what if Jeremy had dumped her, if Craig Peters hadn't called. Her life was still good. She had . . . she had . . . What *did* she have?

Furina. She picked up the cat, who was twining around her legs as she cleaned off her kitchen countertops, reminding Kiley that her cat food bowl was empty. "Who needs men, anyway, right?" she told the cat, running her hands through Furina's soft fur. Of course, employment was another matter. "I am not going to get depressed," she informed the cat, setting her back down on the floor. "And you are not getting anything more until tonight. You're on a diet. Remember?"

Furina rubbed against her leg again. *Pleeease? You think you've got it bad? I haven't had a man in years. The least you can do is let me enjoy a little extra tuna.*

Kiley gave in. "Okay, okay. But you're not getting the whole can. You have to have a little self-control." Like Kiley had exerted over the last of the brownies? Good thing she'd gotten that run in.

The job hunting was done, the condo was clean—what next? She plopped on her couch and frowned at her library book. Then she frowned at the TV. Finally, she glared at the phone. This was ridiculous. Pathetic. She was not going to sit around and wait for a man to call. She needed groceries. She'd go see what she could get for twenty dollars.

She bought the makings for soup, which would get her through the week (and give her something to do when she got home), and all the while her cell phone sat silent and useless in her purse. That night as she readied herself for bed, she averted her eyes whenever she passed the snow globe. It wasn't that she'd lost faith, she told herself. But there was no sense getting her hopes up.

Who was she kidding? She *had* lost faith.

The next day fell into the same familiar pattern. Go for a run. Feel great. Come home and check messages. Lose some of the great feeling. Job hunt, send out résumés, check e-mail, do the tweet 'n' meet thing. Clean some more. Listen for the phone.

Maybe she should call him. They had talked about her designing his Web site. Time was money. Every day he went without a Web site he went without business. She picked up her cell, started to thumb in the number, and then set it down again. She didn't want to look pushy. Or desperate.

She heaved a sigh. What else needed to get done? She'd clean out her closet and take some things to the Goodwill. Perfect. They could always use donations before Christmas.

She not only found items in her closet to donate, she added several paperbacks she'd finished and knew she'd never read again. That was two bags' full now. It felt good to get rid of the clutter, made her feel efficient and organized, like she was clearing the deck for new opportunties. Now, what else could go?

Her eyes fell on the snow globe.

EIGHT

Kiley picked the thing up and frowned at the little angel inside. "You made a fool of me, you know. I should give you away. Or sell you to some other sucker." Of course, the angel had nothing to say for herself. Since she was holding the snow globe, Kiley had to shake it. After the blizzard subsided she saw, once again, Craig Peters and his toyshop. And herself.

Okay, was she delusional? Why hadn't he called?

Who knew? One thing she knew for certain. She couldn't get rid of her treasure, even though she suspected she'd make back at least some of her money if she put it up for auction on eBay. She set it down and resigned herself to hanging in limbo, just like the people inside that glass ball.

Except hanging in limbo wasn't acceptable. She had a life. To prove it she marched to the kitchen and baked some gingerbread cookies. And the next afternoon she went to the food bank and did data entry at the office. If a certain man called and wanted to do something he could just wait his turn. And if he didn't call, oh well. She still had Furina.

She was just walking in the door when her cell phone rang. "Hi," said a male voice. "Remember me, Craig Peters?"

How could she forget?

"I've been thinking about you," he said.

Now her heart started racing like a sprinter in the Olympics. "You have?"

"I had a great time the other night with you at dinner."

"You did?" *Sparkling conversation, Kiley.* She tried again. "I did, too. I've been doing a lot of thinking about your Web site design since then." Okay, she'd been thinking more about him than the Web site, but it wouldn't look cool to say that.

"Want to talk about it while we watch the Christmas boat parade tonight?" he asked.

The popular Northwest tradition had been going on for sixty years. A local cruise line decked one of their boats with Christmas lights, and then with local choirs aboard, visited various waterfront communities, broadcasting concerts to those on shore while passengers enjoyed the live entertainment. Other boats followed, also decorated for the holidays. Greater Seattle residents loved catching the boat parade. Local beaches blazed with bonfires and people hung out to await the floating show.

Kiley had never had a date take her to the boat parade and, yet again, Craig Peters scored points, this time for creativity. "That sounds like fun," she said.

"Dress warm and I'll pick you up about six. By the way, I

meant to call you Sunday, but my mom slipped on an icy patch Sunday morning and broke her arm. I had to take her to the emergency room. The last couple of days I've been helping her out."

So there was the explanation as to why Kiley hadn't heard from him. She hadn't been delusional, and the snow globe was magic. She'd known it all along! Never doubted for a minute. As soon as she was off the phone, she went into hyper-drive, working on Web site ideas and working on herself.

The work paid off. When Craig arrived he took in her Christmas red sweater and her snug jeans and smiled approvingly as she grabbed her coat and hat and mittens. Her hair she'd corralled in a ponytail. Between that and her hat maybe she'd be able to contain it. Maybe.

Richmond Beach, one of the parade's scheduled stops, was alight with an uncountable number of bonfires and people milling around them, drinking cocoa and cider and roasting hot dogs. Kids and dogs darted everywhere along the rocky beach. "This is amazing," Kiley said as they made their way down the hill to the beach.

"Yeah, and somewhere in all this mess is my bro and his friends. If we find them we've got eats waiting."

Amazingly, they did find his brother Jed and a group of his college buddies and girlfriends, who were more than happy to welcome them with steaming cups of hot cider.

Jed, a slightly younger, shorter version of Craig, eyed Kiley appreciatively. "Any time you've had enough of this dweeb, let me know."

Craig pointed a gloved finger at his brother. "Hey, just 'cause you can't find a woman doesn't mean you have to go hitting on my date."

Judging from the way a curvy brunette was watching from the other side of the bonfire, Jed didn't have any problem finding women.

He grinned. "We got hot dogs. You guys hungry?"

"That's why we're here," said Craig. "Free food."

A few minutes later Kiley and Craig had settled on a log with freshly roasted hot dogs and refills of hot cider and were sharing more about their interests.

Their conversation was revealing, showing her more than common interests. As they talked she couldn't help realize how few interests she and Jeremy had really shared.

"So, tell me about your ideas for the Web site," Craig finally said.

She started tentatively, but the excitement on his face encouraged her.

"Awesome," he said when she finished. "Total yes to making the site interactive. I like being able to click on the different toys to go somewhere. And the Kidz Korner with stuff just for kids, that is a really great idea. You know, you are one smart woman."

Kiley tried to look humble. Yes, she was. Well, except for when she'd thought she was in love with Jeremy. What had she been thinking?

"When do you think you can have it up and running?" Craig asked.

"How about by the end of the week?"

"That fast?" He looked impressed.

It wasn't like she had a ton of other work, but she didn't tell him that. Instead she simply smiled and nodded. "I'll send you the link."

"Great. I can send you a check first thing tomorrow."

It was all she could do not to say, "For you, I'd work for free." But she managed to stay professional. "Let's wait to make sure you like it first," she suggested.

"Okay then. Here's to the new Web site," he said, touching his cup of cider to hers.

"To the site," she echoed.

"And to getting to spend more time together," he added. The look in his eyes now had nothing to do with business, and it sent heat rushing through her. "You know, since we're both runners we should run together sometime."

"I'd like that," she said, and felt her heart already taking off at a gallop.

"How about Saturday? No rain or snow predicted. It should be perfect."

"Your store," she protested.

"Doesn't open till ten. I've got time for a run. Eight?"

"Perfect." On so many levels.

They wandered back toward the fire and mingled with the others. Another ten minutes and people began cheering.

"Here they come," Craig said, pointing toward the water. A parade of boats, gaily lit, came into sight. "It doesn't get any better than this," he said, and put an arm around her.

"It sure doesn't," Kiley agreed. But then, later, when he pulled her to him and kissed her, she added, *Oh, yes it does.*

The Web site was finished, approved, and up and running on Friday. It involved few changes, but several conversations. With each one, Kiley fell further and further in love. Craig was enthusiastic and encouraging. And Saturday, after their run, he had a final check for her.

She looked at it. "This is more than we agreed."

"You did more than I ever imagined," he replied. "Hey, we should celebrate."

"Yes, we should," she agreed, smiling. "And I know how."

That evening she made him dinner, serving meat loaf and her mother's fabulous macaroni and cheese because he said he loved comfort food. She also made pie from the blackberries she'd swiped from her mother's freezer.

"This must be a special dinner," her mother had probed.

Kiley had smiled and kissed Mom on the cheek. "I think it is. And when I'm sure, I'll tell you all about it."

"Just take your time," Mom had cautioned.

Kiley had assured her mother that she would, but as she sat across from Craig, watching him tuck into his second helping of pie and ice cream, listening to him talk about his life growing up and his dreams for the future, it was hard to come up with any reason for dragging her feet. He wasn't merely perfect; he was perfect for her.

She fingered the kaleidoscope he'd brought her as a hostess

gift and found herself blurting, "Do you want to have kids?" *Oh, geez, way to scare the man off.*

He set down his fork and looked at her seriously. "Of course. Family is important." He grinned. "Besides, what's the point of having a toy store if you don't have kids to play with? How about you?"

She could feel her cheeks suddenly warming. "Oh, yes," she said with a nod. "But I'm not in any hurry," she added, remembering her mother's cautionary words. "I'm not in a hurry for anything."

He cocked his head to the side and studied her. "What does that mean exactly?"

Then it came out, all the details of her whirlwind romance with Jeremy and his betrayal. "So, I'm taking my time this time around."

Craig nodded slowly. "I can see why. Been there, almost done that. You ever been to Amsterdam?"

She shook her head. She hadn't traveled much. She'd been too busy building a career that had toppled, falling in love with the wrong man, important things like that.

"It's a cool city," said Craig. "Lots of museums, diamond cutters," he added, waggling his eyebrows. "The canals at night are something else. The houses are interesting, too. Not much really, and all close together, but they have these great façades that make 'em look cool." He paused a minute to see if Kiley was following. "A lot of people do that. They build a façade, hoping the other person won't see there isn't much there."

Kiley ran her finger along the rim of her coffee cup. "So you think that's what Jeremy did?"

"Well, it sure doesn't sound like there was much there. Except a lot of bullshit." Craig leaned back in his chair and smiled at her. "But hey, I'm all for taking the long way home. I'm gonna tell you right now, though, Kiley. I'm hooked on you and I can see what we've started going somewhere good."

She smiled. "Me, too."

After a while they moved from the table to the couch, and then from conversation to a kiss. And another and another. She had thought Jeremy was a good kisser, but he was a rank amateur compared to this man. Her lips were buzzing when Craig finally pulled away and looked at her as though she was the most beautiful woman in the world. He picked up a length of unruly curls and twisted them around his finger. "Man, I love your hair."

That was when she decided it was time for show-and-tell. She fetched the snow globe from her bedroom.

"Whoa," he said, sitting up straighter. "That is awesome. Where'd you get it? I've never seen one like it."

"I got it in an antique store." She handed it to him and sat back down on the couch.

He shook it, watching as the snowflakes flew. When they settled, his easy smile changed to an expression of amazement. "That's my shop!"

"You see it?" Was it possible?

"And there's . . . me?" He looked up at her as if to ask if he was crazy. "And you. What the hell?" He began examining the globe. "Is this like those digital photo frames? Did you program it somehow?"

She shook her head. "I didn't do anything."

He frowned. "Okay, I don't get it."

But he'd seen what the snow globe could do. So she told him its story.

When she was finished he simply sat, staring at it. "That's amazing." He looked up at her, his eyes full of wonder.

"If it hadn't been for the snow globe I never would have found you."

"Well, then God bless it," he said heartily. He continued to gaze at it. "What a story to tell our kids." As if realizing what he'd just said, he looked up, his cheeks russet. "Someday," he added. "We don't want to rush into anything."

"No," she said, staring at his lips. "No rushing." But would Valentine's Day be too soon to get engaged?

NINE

Suzanne scowled as she dashed through the freezing rain from the day care to her car, cell phone pressed to her ear. "You just met this man," she scolded Kiley. "You can't know he's the one."

"But I do. I know it sounds crazy," Kiley continued, "but he's perfect. He really, truly is."

She sounded so happy Suzanne wanted to smack her. Kiley lived in la-la land. Did she really think she was going to find Mr. Perfect just like that? As if there was such a thing. Guy came close, but even he had his faults. Like always messing up her house on fight nights, when he and his buddies used watching boxing matches as an excuse to spill beer and pretzel crumbs everywhere. Thank God she could relegate them to the bonus room.

"I'm not saying we're rushing into anything," Kiley continued, "but I know we'll be together for the rest of our lives. I can tell."

"So now you're psychic," Suzanne said with a sneer.

"No. And neither is he, but he saw us in the snow globe, too."

Suzanne rolled her eyes. "He probably just said that to get in your pants. You haven't slept with him, have you?" Sleeping with some man she barely knew was the last thing Kiles needed. She was way too vulnerable.

"Of course not," Kiley said, sounding insulted. "I told you we're taking things slow."

"Just remember you said that," Suzanne cautioned. She plopped her soggy self inside her Lexus and started the engine. She had less than ten minutes to get to the office, where she was meeting a couple looking to find a house on Upper Queen Anne. "I want to meet this guy."

"I didn't say we wanted to take it that slow. I have to make an appointment six months in advance to do anything with you."

"That's not true," said Suzanne, wheeling out onto the street. Oh, great. There was a garbage truck right ahead. Why did these guys have to hog so much of the road? "I've gotta go. Keep me posted on what's going on, okay?"

She hardly gave Kiley time to say goodbye before ending the call and tossing the phone on the front passenger seat. Then she pulled out around the truck and passed him, barely squeaking past a man in a compact tin can heading in the other direction. He commented on her reckless driving with an angry honk.

"Sorry," she muttered. But he'd have done the same. Anyway, she'd had plenty of room to pass, really. The clock on her car dash told her to hurry, hurry, hurry, and she pressed down just a little harder on the gas. Oh, except there was a patrol car farther up the street. She lifted her foot and ground her teeth. Why was she always running late?

Of course, the answer to that was easy. She had way too much on her plate. Today was no exception. Between showing four houses, following up on a listing lead, picking up the signs for the holiday open house, and checking on two deals that were in escrow, her workday was full. Then Bryn had her ballet lesson at five. After that it would be time to go home and make dinner. Or maybe she'd pick up a pizza on the way, even though she'd done that three days ago.

But that couldn't be helped. She'd planned to make a nice meal until a couple called dying to see a condo that had just come on the market. They both worked during the day and had wanted to see it that evening. She'd barely had time to grab a slice before running back out the door.

Tonight the calendar was clear after ballet, but the thought of slaving away in the kitchen made her shudder. Guy usually cooked on Friday nights. Maybe he'd trade.

She parked in front of the office and put in a quick call to suggest it.

"Wait a minute," he protested. "You pulled that one on me last week and then on Friday you were too tired to cook." He politely refrained from mentioning that she had also been too tired for sex.

"I promise I won't back out this Friday," she said. "I'll make Indian," she added to sweeten the pot.

He heaved a long-suffering sigh. "All right. Deal. But it's

going to be spaghetti. You're not the only one who comes home pooped, you know."

"But I'm the only one who comes home pooped and has to take Bryn to ballet." Oh, yeah, he'd done that for her last week, too. Bad argument.

"Yeah?"

"Okay, never mind. I forgot about last week. Come on, Guy, don't give me a hard time here."

"All right, all right."

"I love you," she cooed. It always helped to remind him why he so often went the extra mile.

"I love you, too," he said, "even though you're working both of us into an early grave."

She let the comment go but she hung up with a frown. What did he expect? They had a big home improvement loan to pay off.

Loan or no loan, though, they'd probably work just as hard. Guy loved his job as a systems analyst and would have worked at his company for free. And she felt the same about what she did. Beautiful houses—she breathed, ate, and dreamed them. She always felt like she'd done something good when she helped a family find their dream home, the place where they could build happy lives in a lovely setting. A nice house was the most important gift a person could give herself, and the nicest gift she could give her family. Sometimes Suzanne suspected Guy didn't get that.

She climbed out of the car just as Melanie and James Cox pulled up behind her.

"Hi," she called, hurrying up to them. "I think I've found the perfect place for you." It came with a view and a high price tag, but it was worth every penny.

Melanie and James loved the house and agreed. So did another couple who were looking with her archrival Sasha Hearst over at Windermere, which meant Suzanne had a bidding war on her hands. She hated bidding wars. Except when her people won.

Melanie and James didn't win. They dropped out after offering a measly thousand dollars over asking price, even though Suzanne tried her best to convince them that they could well afford to go up yet another five. But James was conservative and Melanie was a wimp. Suzanne pasted a smile on her face and assured them that she'd find something else for them that would be equally wonderful, even though she knew she wouldn't. That had been the perfect house and they'd let it get away.

To top off her day she learned that one of her deals wasn't going to make it through escrow. Ugh.

But that was the real estate business, she reminded herself as she left the office. Tomorrow would be better.

Still, she felt grumpy as she sat on a cold metal chair at the Happy Feet dance studio, watching her daughter and a dozen other five- and six-year-old ballerinas do their *battement tendus*. The dance recital was right around the corner and the person Suzanne had paid to make Bryn's costume hadn't even started it yet. Frustrating as she found this, Suzanne understood. Everyone was overextended, especially with the holidays looming. Holidays. Shopping. She hadn't even begun.

Simply thinking about all she had to do started a headache blooming. She reached into her purse, pulled out her little bottle of Excedrin, and popped one. She used to need water to wash them down. Now she swallowed them dry.

The girls began to work on their dance number for the recital. They were all going to be sugar plum fairies and Bryn was so excited it was almost all she talked about. The only subject that took precedence over fairyhood was the hope that Santa would bring her a puppy for Christmas.

Suzanne had already informed her daughter that Santa didn't carry puppies in his sleigh. They might fall out and get hurt. Bryn had assured her mother that Santa's sleigh came equipped with seat belts. Who had told her that? Probably Guy. He was the moving force behind this, sure that every kid needed a dog. Well, every mom didn't need a dog, and this mom needed one like she needed to take up mud wrestling. Bryn would get a pretty stuffed puppy to put on her bed. That kind of dog never peed in the house.

The dance lesson was over and Bryn hopped up to her. "Did you see me, Mommy?"

"Yes," Suzanne lied. Actually, she'd gotten so preoccupied that she hadn't seen a thing. But she knew she was safe in adding, "You were great."

Bryn beamed and jumped up and down. "Can we get ice cream?"

On the days when Guy took their daughter to ballet they always stopped on the way home for ice cream, thus succeeding in spoiling Bryn's appetite for dinner.

"Not tonight, sweetie. We have to get home. Daddy's making dinner."

By the time they got home the aroma of Italian spices filled the house.

"Daddy, we're home!" Bryn called. She started to race across the entryway.

"Ah-ah! Shoes," Suzanne reminded her.

Bryn fell down and quickly pulled off her shoes, tossing them in the general direction of the wicker shoe basket Suzanne kept by the door, then raced off down the hallway toward the kitchen.

Suzanne followed at a slower pace. She was suddenly so tired she barely had enough energy to admire the antique table in the entryway or the shine of her highly polished hardwood floors and how well they set off the new rug as she walked past her living room. It looked exactly like something out of *Better Homes and Gardens*. In fact, the whole house looked that way and good looks didn't just happen. She had worked hard making the house into something beautiful, a real step up from her childhood home.

Step? This wasn't a mere step up; it was an entire staircase. The rickety mess of a house Suzanne had grown up in had been nothing to bring friends home to. Not so here. Suzanne could entertain Martha Stewart herself.

"Hi, babe," Guy greeted her. He had shed his suit and was standing at the stove in jeans and his old University of Washington sweatshirt, stirring his favorite brand of bottled spaghetti sauce. He'd rumpled his dark hair in the process of changing and hadn't bothered to unrumple it. Because he was so darned handsome, the look fit him well. Two glasses of red wine sat next to him on the counter and he held one out to her. "You look pooped. Not a good day in the real estate biz?"

He leaned down and kissed her and she took the wine. "You could say that. I found the perfect house for the Coxes and they wimped out." She shook her head sadly at the memory of the couple's foolishness.

"Bidding war, huh?"

"It's hard to have a war when one side surrenders after the first shot's been fired."

"Well, maybe they're on a budget."

"They could afford it," Suzanne scoffed.

"Maybe they don't want to sink everything they own into a house. Maybe they have other priorities."

Was that some kind of hidden message? She studied her husband, but he didn't give her much to study.

She watched as he shoved a handful of angel hair pasta into a pot of boiling water. "What could be more important than having a nice home for your family?"

He shrugged. "Everyone has a different definition of nice, babe."

"I guess," she conceded. "But they were fools. That was the ideal house for them and they let it get away. The Turner deal is going south on me, too." She started pulling plates out of the cupboard. "What a day."

"I know all my steps, Daddy," piped Bryn, and demonstrated.

Guy smiled fondly at her. "Good for you, princess." He ruffled her hair and then set to work draining pasta.

"Grammy is going to be so proud when she comes up to visit," added Suzanne. Now, why had she mentioned her mother's upcoming Christmas visit? Just the thought of the mess that would come with her was enough to destroy all the good work of the Excedrin: Popsicle sticks and glue everywhere, chaos in the kitchen 24-7, tacky popcorn strings—ugh. Her mother was like Martha Stewart's trashy cousin and, of course, she'd want to spread the love. Well, she wasn't touching the tree. Suzanne would make that clear. Hopefully, since she wasn't coming up until the day before Christmas she couldn't cause too much of a problem. Please, God, let that be true.

"If I dance nice maybe Santa will bring me a puppy," said Bryn.

"Oh, sweetie, Santa doesn't have any puppies scheduled for this neighborhood," Suzanne said. Somehow the puppy message wasn't getting through.

"But I asked," Bryn said, determined as ever to win this argument.

"Yes, but there are only so many puppies to go around. And I think the last delivery will be in . . . Virginia."

"What's Virginia?" asked Bryn.

"Someplace that's not here," replied Suzanne. She could feel Guy's gaze on her and turned to see him looking at her with disappointment. "What?" she said defensively. He shook his head and turned back to the spaghetti, a sure sign that they would be discussing this later. Goody.

TEN

Sure enough, later that evening, after Bryn was in bed and Suzanne and Guy were settled on the couch with a fire in the gas fireplace and another glass of wine, he said, "I think we should reconsider the dog thing. You know the Lovgrins are trying to find homes for those foster puppies."

How could she not know? Every time she came to the day care provider's house to pick up Bryn she had to see the smelly beasts.

"Golden labs are great dogs for kids," said Guy.

She set down her wineglass and sat up and frowned at him. "Who are you kidding? I saw the trailer for *Marley and Me*. Anyway, just because Bryn wants a dog it doesn't mean she has to have one. My God, I'd like a Jag for Christmas. Are you going to run out and get one for me?"

"Not after all the money we've spent on this place," he teased.

"We don't have time in our life for a dog," she reminded him. Sometimes it seemed like they barely had time in their life for each other. That thought bothered her so she shied away from it. "Who'd housebreak it?"

"We both could," he said, pulling her back to him.

"Nice of you to volunteer me."

He grinned, unrepentant.

"Guy, we're never around. It wouldn't be fair to the animal."

Now his grin got bigger. "That's changing."

A sick feeling settled over her. What horrible news was he about to announce? Was he quitting to run a home business? "What?"

"Remember I told you I was going to talk to Jameson about working from home a couple days a week? Well, I did. Starting in January I'll be home on Mondays and Fridays."

"And what about the other days?" she argued.

"You're around in the mornings sometimes."

"And sometimes I'm not. And on the days I'm not, a dog will chew up shoes, rip sofa cushions, and gnaw my new rug to bits."

"Not if we get a baby gate and a crate."

Which the thing would turn into a doggie bathroom.

"Let's at least think about it," Guy urged.

"I'll think," she said, "but not very hard and not very long. Bryn's too young for a pet anyway. We should wait until she's older and more responsible."

"I had a dog by the time I was her age," he argued, and kissed her ear.

And he'd had dogs ever since. He'd grown up with the sloppy, smelly things. In fact, he'd had a dog before he met her. It was an ugly mutt. She'd seen pictures of Guy and Morris the Mutt posed on hiking trails, in boats, on his front porch. They were just dating when Morris finally expired of old age, and Guy had mourned the dog as if it were a child. He'd always said he'd never get another and that had been fine with her, but now, with Bryn asking, he was teetering on the edge of dog ownership again, ready to take her over with him.

"Can we please not talk about this anymore tonight?" she pleaded. "I am so tired."

"Tired? There's a surprise." He started to move away.

She stopped him. "But I'm not that tired," she murmured, setting aside her wine. Actually, all she wanted to do was fall into bed and sleep for a hundred years, but she could put off sleep long enough to show her husband some love. And distract him from talking about dogs.

It was harder to distract herself. Her guilty mother's conscience continued to prod her. She didn't spend enough time with her daughter. The least she could do was let the child have a pet. She told her conscience to shut up. Several times. Yes, Bryn wanted a dog, but once the novelty wore off it would be Suzanne taking care of it. A stuffed puppy would be perfect. She and Bryn could play with it together. Maybe they'd name it Morris and Guy could play with it, too. Ha.

Wednesday was a great day. A miracle occurred and Suzanne found another perfect house for the Coxes, and it was a steal. They had learned their lesson, and this time they didn't dither on price and won the prize. Later, when Kiley called, Suzanne was in a great mood.

"I have a prezzie for you," said Kiley.

"I thought we weren't going to do presents this year," Suzanne protested as she sorted through the pile of papers on her desk. Not that she minded exchanging presents, but she hadn't had time to shop.

"I know," said Kiley, "but this is something I really want you to have."

It was sweet of Kiles, but dang, now Suzanne had one more thing on her to-do list. She'd race to Nordstrom's on the way to pick up Bryn and get something. Maybe she'd give Kiley a gift certificate. She could use some new clothes. While she was at it she'd get one for Allison, too.

Problem solved, deep breath. "Okay, why don't you come over for dinner Friday? I'm making Indian."

"Can't. I've got a date."

Suzanne cringed. "With the snow globe dude?"

"That would be the one. We're taking his mom to the living Christmas tree concert."

Suzanne could hear the smile in her friend's voice. Oh, boy. Kiles was sliding right over the edge of the romantic cliff. Suzanne just knew it.

"I thought I'd swing by tonight on my way to Allison's."

"Oh. What are you guys doing?"

"We're making fudge."

Suzanne liked fudge. How come she wasn't invited?

"We'd have told you except you've been so busy lately," Kiley added.

"I'd have made time."

"Well, then, want to come?"

She watched the fingers of rain slithering down her office window and shivered. This would be a perfect evening to hang out in Allison's kitchen, surrounded by the aroma of melting chocolate. But . . . "I can't," she admitted. "I have to show a house at seven-thirty."

"I'll stop by at six," Kiley said, her tone of voice adding, *See? That's why you didn't get invited to make fudge.*

Suzanne hung up and drummed her fingers on her desktop. What else had she heard in Kiley's voice, a little bit of judgment? As if it was a bad thing that she worked for a living?

Her conversation with Kiley left Suzanne feeling out of sorts, but she pasted on a polite smile for April Lovgrin when she picked up Bryn. The Lovgrins' home was kid heaven, full of toys and pets. The Lovgrins also took in foster puppies, keeping them until they got adopted. This had seemed like a plus when Suzanne first put Bryn in day care there. Now it was a thorn in her side. Every day, just like today, Bryn greeted her, holding a roly-poly puppy. Was April putting her up to this?

"Look, Mommy," said Bryn, holding up the pup. "His name is Happy."

Wasn't that the name of one of the seven dwarves? Messy would have been more accurate.

April stood behind Bryn in jeans and a green sweatshirt, a Santa hat shoved over her auburn hair. "We only have two left.

This one and his sister," she said, giving Suzanne yet another chance to stake a claim.

"I'm sure you'll find a nice home for him," said Suzanne.

"Guy was pretty interested in this little fella," said April.

Guy and April were in cahoots. "We're not quite ready for a dog yet." The puppy wriggled in Bryn's arms and lapped her cheek with a sloppy dog tongue. *Eeew.* "Don't let him lick you like that," said Suzanne. "He probably just finished licking his bottom. Here, honey, put him down. We have to go."

Bryn set the puppy down with reluctance. Of course, it tried to follow them, bounding after Suzanne like she was a giant dog toy.

"No, no, doggie, get away," said Suzanne, giving it a nudge with the toe of her high heel.

April made a face and snatched the stupid thing up as if she'd just rescued it from Cruella De Vil.

Okay, so Suzanne's shoe had a bit of a pointed toe. She hadn't hurt the dog. Still, she felt her cheeks warming. "Don't want him to get out and get hit by a car," she explained.

April just nodded.

Suzanne felt like a dog-beating monster now. "Well, thanks for watching Bryn," she said, injecting extra appreciation in her voice. "You're the best."

April's smile didn't thaw, so Suzanne got the heck out of there.

"Can we write a letter to Santa tonight?" asked Bryn as they drove away.

"Another letter?" Oh, geez. She already knew what was going to be in it.

Bryn nodded. "I want to ask him for Happy."

"I think Santa already has a home in mind for Happy."

Bryn's lower lip jutted out and a tear slipped down her cheek.

Great, thought Suzanne miserably. First she'd kicked a dog. Now she'd made her daughter cry.

But she hadn't kicked the dog. She'd just nudged it away. And it was really Guy's fault that her daughter was crying. He was the one who put the idea of a puppy into Bryn's head in the first place. *Maybe Santa will bring you a puppy.* What was that about? Maybe Santa would bring Guy a lump of coal. He sure deserved it.

Kiley arrived promptly at six, just as Suzanne was serving the frozen pizza she'd picked up at QFC on the way home.

"Want some?" Guy offered. "There's plenty."

Kiley shook her head. "Thanks, but I already ate. I can't stay long, anyway."

Because she was off to make fudge while Suzanne was off to try and make a sale. Kiley looked so happy, so relaxed, like life was wonderful. For one delusional moment, Suzanne found herself feeling a tiny bit jealous. A nice, fat commission would buy an entire house full of fudge, she reminded herself.

Kiley set a green foil gift bag bursting with gold tissue paper on the kitchen table. "Open it."

"This is pretty," said Suzanne. She loved presents, loved pretty wrapping paper almost more than what lay under it, and she always coordinated her present wrapping with her Christmas tree decorations. This year she intended to dress her tree, her house, and her family to the nines.

"Come on, open it," urged Kiley.

Suzanne fished inside the bag. She knew what it was the minute her fingers closed around it. *Oh, no.* Sure enough.

"Hey, a snow globe," said Guy. "That's a great one."

And it would look gorgeous on her mantel. The only catch was, Kiley would expect her to see something in it. "I can't take this," Suzanne protested. And not just because of the woo-woo factor. "You paid a small fortune for it."

"Yes, but what I got from it was priceless. I think I'm supposed to pass it on."

"But I don't need anything," said Suzanne.

Bryn held out her hands. "I want to see it."

Suzanne moved her daughter's dish out of the way. "Okay, hold it very carefully," she said, and hovered.

"It's so pretty," whispered Bryn in awe.

"Shake it," said Guy. He leaned over and helped her.

Suzanne held her breath, fearing her daughter would drop the snow globe. Or, worse, Kiley would start seeing things.

The snow settled, revealing the same little village and the angel. Good. Safe.

Bryn gave a gasp of delight. "A puppy!"

A what?

ELEVEN

"Look, Daddy!" cried Bryn.

Guy grinned. "Well, whaddya know."

Suzanne looked, too. There was nothing in the snow globe but an angel window-shopping outside a toyshop.

"It looks just like Happy," Bryn said, exercising her imagination to the max.

"Oh, look. He's found a home in Virginia," said Suzanne.

"No, he hasn't, Mommy," insisted Bryn. "That's our house."

"It sure is," agreed Guy, smiling. "There's our red front door and the Christmas wreath Mommy just got."

Okay, enough encouraging false hope, Suzanne thought irritably. "What do you know! A house in Virginia that's just like ours," she said, giving her husband a look that warned retribution if he didn't cease his naughty behavior.

Meanwhile, Kiley the Typhoid Mary of Christmas was beaming cluelessly.

Bryn shook the thing again, watching it in delight.

"What else do you see? I think I see a new doll," said Suzanne.

Bryn was focused on the snow globe. "I just see Happy," she said matter-of-factly.

"Well," said Suzanne briskly, "I bet the puppy in there is tired." She took the snow globe from Bryn's reluctant hands. "We'll put him on the mantel so he can go to sleep, okay?"

"Can't he sleep with me?" begged Bryn.

"No, baby," said Suzanne. "This is very old. It might break. We'll put it on the mantel where it will be safe."

"Can I see Happy in it again tomorrow?" asked Bryn.

I hope not. "Maybe," said Suzanne. "Or you might see something else. You never know."

Kiley stood, saying, "I'd better get going."

Yeah, fine. Run now that the damage is done.

"It looks like you guys are getting Bryn a dog for Christmas after all," Kiley as she took her coat from the hall closet.

"Uh, no."

Kiley's brows knit. "But Bryn saw—"

"What she wanted to see," finished Suzanne. "The dog thing is not happening."

"Oh." Kiley looked nonplussed for a moment. "But Guy saw it."

"Guy was playing along. He wants a dog almost as much as Bryn. Sorry to burst your bubble."

"I can tell," said Kiley with a scowl.

Now she'd offended Kiles. The part of Suzanne that felt bad was quickly devoured by its sensible twin, which said,

The sooner Kiles learns that grown-ups do not live in la-la land the better.

Still, she only wanted to be the voice of reason, not the Grinch. "I'm sorry I can't make fudge with you guys. Save me some?"

"Sure." Kiley's voice was frosty.

Suzanne laid a hand on her arm and added, "I do love the snow globe. It's beautiful and it will look lovely on my fireplace mantel."

"It's not just a decoration, Suz," Kiley said, looking at her earnestly. "I hope you give it a chance to do something for you."

"I don't know what it's going to do," said Suzanne. "There's nothing I need." Well, money. That always came in handy. Now Kiley was looking so disappointed Suzanne added, "Except my friends. Don't be mad. Okay?"

Kiley sighed and nodded. "Okay."

After she left Suzanne found herself feeling like she had failed some secret test. She was a hard-working realist; therefore she didn't qualify for the fudge reward. *We'd have told you except you've been so busy lately.* The implication: You're too busy for your friends. Then there was Guy's crack the night before. *Tired? There's a surprise.* As if she got worn out on purpose. What was wrong with everyone these days? This was a crazy time of year. What was so shocking about the fact that she was busy? And tired?

She'd make a superhuman effort to go by Kiley's place after she'd shown that house. She could have her clients through in under an hour.

Or not. Her clients loved the house and wanted to make an offer immediately. A good real estate broker didn't say, "Tell you what. I have to go make fudge with my girlfriends, but I'll be on that first thing tomorrow." So she drew up their offer. Of course, the seller counteroffered. So by the time Suzanne and the listing agent were done it was after nine and she was pooped. But very satisfied. She'd closed the deal. She'd found her clients the perfect house and she'd made a perfectly respectable chunk of change. That trumped making fudge any day, even at Christmas.

Still, hanging out with Kiley and Allison would have been fun.

She came home to find Guy up in the bonus room, flopped on the leather couch, watching a remake of *A Christmas Carol*. He looked up at her and said, "Congratulations," robbing her of the opportunity to announce her success.

"How'd you know I made the sale?"

"The smug smile."

She lifted his feet and plopped down on the end of the couch, letting him use her lap as a footstool. "Well, then, since you were smart enough to figure out that I made the sale you should also be smart enough to be praising me for my brilliance."

He smiled. "You're brilliant, babe. Are we rich yet?"

Not with the bills they had.

"Your daughter asked for a puppy when she said her prayers tonight," Guy informed her.

First Santa, now God—Bryn was really bringing in the

heavy artillery. Suzanne had found it easy enough to explain why Santa couldn't come through. God was another matter. And Kiley hadn't helped with that darned snow globe. Which reminded Suzanne: "Did you have to say you saw a puppy in the snow globe?"

"I call it as I see it," he said with a shrug.

Suzanne pointed a finger at him. "No way did you see anything. You just said that to encourage Bryn and to back me into a corner."

Guy dropped his smile and studied her intently. "Suz, what's happened to you?"

"What is that supposed to mean?" she bristled. Nothing had happened to her. She was the same person she'd always been.

"What happened to just working part-time? That was all you were going to do. Remember?"

"I can't help it if my business has grown," she said. She shoved his feet off her lap and stood up. "I'm working really hard to give us a nice home, Guy, and you don't seem to appreciate it."

"No," he corrected her. "You're working hard to give us a nice house, and I never said I wanted that."

"I can't believe what I'm hearing," she said, throwing up her hands.

He heaved a long-suffering sigh. "I understand that you want things nice, babe, but come on. You've turned into friggin' Martha Stewart on steroids."

She was working her fingers to the bone and this was the thanks she got. "Well, thank you for your appreciation," she snapped. "I guess next time I want to celebrate making a sale I'll do it with someone at work," she added, and left. *There, chew on that.*

She took a bubble bath, and then went to bed with the latest issue of *Better Homes and Gardens*. She didn't find out whether Guy had given any thought to what she said because she fell asleep before he came to bed, and by the time she woke up the next morning he had already left for work.

That was just as well, she decided. There really was no sense in picking up the potentially explosive discussion. Better to let sleeping puppies lie.

But as she got ready for her day a new concern niggled at her. She'd thought that Guy was as happy with their life as she was. Surely their happiness didn't depend on whether or not they got a dog. And surely he didn't really want her to scale back when she was doing so well with her career.

Every marriage has issues, she reminded herself as she dropped Bryn off at day care.

And every mother has parenting challenges, she added later, when Bryn pouted all the way home after Suzanne told her they couldn't bring Happy with them.

"We don't have a bed for him," Suzanne had pointed out. "He'd have nowhere to sleep."

Of course, Bryn had a solution for that. "He can sleep with me."

Now, there was a disgusting thought. "We don't have a dog dish or dog food or a flea collar," added Suzanne.

"Let's get them now," Bryn suggested.

"Bryn, we are not bringing Happy home," Suzanne had finally said.

Bryn had crossed her arms and scowled just the way Suzanne used to when she was a little girl. Then she'd added tears, and they were still rolling down her cheeks when they walked through the front door.

"Whoa, what's this?" Guy greeted them.

He was already out of his suit and in his stocking feet, wearing his favorite ratty sweats in honor of fight night. Another hour and the bonus room would be a rocking place, with men shouting at the TV screen, punching the air with their fists, and spilling beer everywhere. The perfect ending to a perfect day.

"Mommy won't let me have Happy," sobbed Bryn. "And now Santa won't bring him."

Not if he doesn't want to come down the chimney and get barbecued by a roaring fire.

Guy frowned at Suzanne. It wasn't your normal, garden-variety frown. It was something worse, tinged with an emotion Suzanne had rarely seen, at least not when he was looking at her: disgust.

She realized she'd taken a step backward. She stopped and put up her chin. "There is more than one person living here, you know."

"Yes," said Guy. "There is." He picked up Bryn and carried her out to the kitchen. "Don't worry, Brynnie, Santa will have something cool for you. Hey, how about some leftover spaghetti?"

Suzanne slammed down her briefcase. Fine. Make her the bad

guy just because she was trying to be practical. And, speaking of practical, Guy hadn't even removed Bryn's shoes, Suzanne fumed as she slipped off her heels. He'd done that deliberately, to irritate her, she was sure. She followed them to the kitchen where Guy was already heating spaghetti in the microwave—a small bowl for Bryn, nothing for his wife, the puppy hater. No wineglass sat on the counter, either.

Fine. She could pour her own wine. She pulled a glass from the cupboard and a bottle of white wine from the fridge.

"There you go, kidlet," Guy said, setting the bowl in front of Bryn. "How about some milk?"

Bryn was still sniffling. "I want Happy."

"Yeah, well, sometimes Mrs. Claus makes it hard for Santa to come through," Guy muttered.

"Maybe that's because Mrs. Claus knows who will wind up doing most of the work," said Suzanne.

"Mrs. Claus doesn't know squat," Guy said flatly. The doorbell rang. "That's probably Clay. Looks like you're on duty now," he added, and left her alone with her sniffling daughter and a traitorous conscience that was turning guilty.

Oh, this is ridiculous, she thought. Sometimes kids need to learn to take no for an answer and now is one of those times.

"I saw Happy in the snow globe," Bryn said, and gave the table leg an angry kick.

Suzanne removed her daughter's shoes. "Finish your spaghetti, sweetie."

She went to the front hall and deposited the shoes in the basket. Guy had vanished upstairs with his buddy for a night of testosterone overload. That was fine with her. She hoped he knocked himself out shadowboxing. Frowning, she straightened the mess of keys and receipts Guy had dumped on the entryway table. Dogs. Bah, humbug. It would have been nice if the snow globe had produced something worthwhile, like her and Guy and Bryn all strolling along a downtown street window-shopping, or at the Sheraton enjoying the gingerbread village display. Or a glimpse of the living room all done up for Christmas as proof that the decorator would get to her before New Year's Day.

With everything in place once more she turned and started back for the kitchen. She'd give Bryn a bubble bath and then they'd read a story. That would distract her from her dog fixation.

But Bryn was no longer in the kitchen. As Suzanne passed the living room door she spotted her daughter balancing on tip-toe on the arm of the wingback chair Suzanne had positioned by the fireplace, one hand on the mantel, the other on the snow globe. And the chair was just about to tip.

"Bryn!"

Of course, startling her daughter was the equivalent of try-ing to make one final addition to a teetering tower of blocks. Bryn gave a guilty start and the chair began to go.

A shot of adrenaline gave Suzanne superhuman speed and strength and she leaped the rest of the way across the room. She managed to catch her daughter but she also caught the side of the glass-topped coffee table, lost her balance, and came down on a very twisted ankle before winding up splayed on the floor, Bryn on top of her. As all this happened she heard glass shatter and she felt a lightning bolt of pain flash up her leg. She saw stars, she saw the chair tumble away, saw the upended coffee table and her daughter's startled expression, and the snow globe in Bryn's hands churning up a white cloud.

Hitting the floor knocked the breath out of Suzanne. Pain made it difficult to regain it. Good God, she'd thought labor pains were bad, but this—there were no waves to peak and subside. This pain kept relentlessly pounding up her ankle.

"Get Daddy," she finally gasped.

With a wail of terror, Bryn set down the snow globe and ran off.

Suzanne closed her eyes against both the pain and the scene emerging as the snow settled inside the glass globe.

Nooooo.

TWELVE

Bryn ran from the room, crying, "Daddy, Daddy!"

Suzanne gritted her teeth and sat up. The sight of her ankle was enough to make her light-headed and sick and she lay back down with a cry. No human ankle was meant to look like that.

Bryn had barely left before Suzanne heard the pounding of feet. Guy's friend Clay stopped at the door and gawked.

Guy rushed past him and knelt by her. "Suz, my God. What happened?"

"Bryn was climbing on the chair and fell. I think I'm going to be sick." *On the carpet. Noooo.* Suzanne clutched her stomach and willed the nausea back.

Bryn hovered in the doorway next to Clay. "I just wanted to see Happy," she said, and burst into fresh tears.

"It's okay, Brynnie," said Guy. "Suz, baby, we'd better get you to the emergency room."

"Yeah, that looks bad," Clay said as he picked up the crying Bryn.

"That damned snow globe," Suzanne growled, brushing tears from her cheek. "I wish Kiley had never brought it." The thing had been like Pandora's box, loosing all kinds of troubles on them. If they'd never seen it Bryn would have dropped her puppy fixation, Guy wouldn't have been mad, and Suzanne wouldn't have wound up with a foot that looked like it belonged on an elephant. And her coffee table would be in one piece.

"Let's get you to the car," Guy said to her.

"Bryn needs to go to bed," she protested.

"I can handle it, huh?" said Clay, giving Bryn a toss and making her smile for the first time since the accident. "Want Uncle Clay to put you to bed?"

Bryn sniffled and nodded. "Is my mommy going to be okay?"

"Of course, she is," said Guy. "Okay, babe. Up we go."

Suzanne tried not to groan as Guy carried her out and settled her in the car, but the pain was excruciating. No one ever died of a sprained ankle, she told herself, though it just felt like her injury was going to kill her. If she didn't get something for the pain soon she was going to gnaw off her leg.

The ride to Group Health Ballard took only minutes but it felt like hours, and the examination and X-rays were nearly unbearable. She had obviously angered the patron saint of dogs.

The final verdict was worse than anticipated. She hadn't simply sprained her ankle; she'd managed to break it. As soon as the swelling went down she'd be in a big, ugly cast. How was she supposed to drive with a broken ankle? How could she show houses? How could she do *anything*? Why the heck, if something had to get broken, couldn't it have been the snow globe?

When she finally came home it was with crutches and a splint. And, thank God, pain pills. Those not only took away the pain, they made it feel like not such a big deal that she suddenly had no life. Who cared, she decided as she floated away on clouds of drug-induced comfort and joy.

The next morning Suzanne awoke to the smell of coffee and an urgent message from her ankle that it was time for more painkillers. She spotted the bottle on her nightstand and raided it, then lay back against the pillows with a groan. While waiting for the meds to take effect she occupied her time listing the many ways she would destroy the snow globe once she was up and moving again: throw it off the Aurora Bridge, donate it to some gun club to use for target practice, beat it to smithereens with her crutches. That last one appealed the most. The enjoyment would last longer.

The pills kicked in and she decided it was safe to try and get up. A glance at the clock told her it was almost nine. Sheesh. She should be on her way to the office. Instead she was only on her way to the bathroom. It wasn't an easy trip with one working leg and, once there, she managed to drop one of her crutches and knock her fancy soap bottle off the counter. Of course it broke, sending a puddle of soap across the floor. Great. The way her luck had been going she'd slip on it and break her other ankle.

She managed to escape slipping on the soap and had just gotten back in bed when Guy arrived, bearing a mug of coffee. "I thought I heard you."

She frowned. "It was probably hard not to. I'm sure I sounded like a rhino."

"But a small one," he assured her, handing over the mug.

"Thanks," she murmured, then nodded to the clock on her nightstand. "You didn't go to work?"

"I took the day off."

Both of them missing work. Great. "Sorry. By the way, I managed to knock over the soap."

He shrugged. "Not a problem. I'll take care of it."

"What a mess everything is," she said miserably.

"It could be worse," he said. "Bryn could have been hurt. That was some rescue you managed, Supermom, leaping over the coffee table in a single bound."

"Not much of a leap considering the fact that I knocked it over," she said with a frown. "How on earth am I going to do anything?" Right before Christmas—could she have picked a worse time for this?

"Don't worry. Help is on the way," Guy said from the bathroom.

She could hear the sounds of glass scraping on the floor. What was he using to clean that up? One of her good towels, of course.

"You hired someone?" she called. Where had he found somebody so quickly?

He reappeared in the doorway bearing a towel full of mess. "This help is free."

She got a sudden uneasy feeling in the pit of her stomach. "Free? Who?"

"Your mother. She's already on her way up from Portland."

"My . . . ? Oh, no."

Suzanne knew what that meant. Corny movies on TV every

night, including a command screening of *It's a Wonderful Life,* the dreaded tacky home-crafted decorations, and, of course, a lecture on what a great blessing in disguise Suzanne's broken ankle was. Now she could take time to savor the joys of the season. As if Suzanne didn't already.

But she didn't savor the season the way her mother did, which meant she didn't do it right. Like all daughters since the dawn of time, she didn't measure up to her mother's expectations.

She could hear her mother now. "You don't need a decorator, dear, not when we can cut out snowflakes and paint Santas on the windows." Just the thought of what the house would look like under her mother's reign was enough to make Suzanne shudder.

"Why did you have to call her?" Suzanne groaned.

"I didn't," Guy said. "She happened to call last night and Clay told her what happened. She called again after you were in bed and insisted on coming. What could I do?"

"You could have told her we're fine," Suzanne said irritably.

"Yeah? You're on pain pills and crutches. Just how fine are we?"

"Perfectly," Suzanne insisted, even though she knew it was a lie.

"You'll be better if you get some help and some rest," Guy said. He leaned over and gave her a kiss on the forehead. "The more you rest the faster you'll heal."

"What's Bryn doing?" she asked.

"Watching a Disney princess movie. So I'm going to check

on my e-mail and make some calls," he said, heading for the door. "Do you want breakfast before I start?"

The last thing she wanted was food. She shook her head.

"Okay. Call or bang on the floor with your crutch if you need something," he said, and left.

What she needed he couldn't bring her. She glared at her useless foot. This was grossly unfair.

The phone rang. She snapped it open and said a pissy, "Hello."

"It's nine-thirty. Are you on your way?" asked Julie, her partner. Julie was the office's other top seller. She and Suzanne had dreamed up the holiday home tour the year before, and with their combined flair and drive it had been a huge success. This year they anticipated twice the turnout and twice the business.

Of course Suzanne was supposed to have been in the office by now and they should have been working on the home tour. "I broke my ankle," she said bitterly. But the cursed snow globe was just fine.

"Oh, no."

"Oh, yes. Right now I'm in bed getting high on painkillers," said Suzanne, smoothing the comforter over her legs.

"Gosh, I'm sorry. Do you need anything?"

"Only a new foot."

There was a moment's silence on the other end of the line, followed by a tentative, "Um, how long are you going to be in bed?"

"Just a couple of days," Suzanne promised. "I'll be up and around by the tour. Don't worry."

"Well, okay," said Julie, sounding doubtful. "But if you're not I can pull in Maria. We can handle it."

And the sales that went along with it. "I'll be fine," Suzanne assured both Julie and herself.

Or not. It seemed all she was good for was sleeping, and when the painkillers started to wear off she wanted to scream. The crutches were instruments of torture and the thought of going downstairs made her shudder. She could just see herself falling and breaking her neck. Ugh.

Bryn was restless and alternated between wanting to play Candy Land and wanting to know why Happy couldn't come live with them. "Because that's how it is," Suzanne finally said wearily.

Her mother arrived early that afternoon. She floated into the bedroom in a cloud of cheap gardenia perfume, wearing her latest discount store bargains. She was still living on a teacher's salary, but she was an empty-nester now and could afford better clothes. Still, she insisted on dressing like she hadn't a penny to her name no matter how many gift cards her daughter sent her.

"Who do I need to impress?" she always said.

No one, obviously. Certainly not a man. Mary Madison had been a widow way too long to ever think about adding a new man to her life. Although maybe she should. Then she'd have someone besides her children to drive crazy.

She took one look at Suzanne and her face filled with pity. "Oh, my poor girl." She perched on the edge of the bed and laid a gentle hand on Suzanne's brow as if Suzanne were dying of a fever.

All right. Maybe it hadn't been such a bad idea to call her.

"How do you feel?" she asked.

"Rotten," said Suzanne. Frustrated. Grumpy.

"Well, I'm going to make you some good, old-fashioned vegetable soup. You used to love that when you were sick."

Her mother's vegetable soup—the finest restaurant in Seattle couldn't touch it. "That would be great," said Suzanne.

Now Bryn was in the room, squealing, "Grammy!" and running pell-mell toward her grandmother.

Mom intercepted her just before she could crash onto the bed. "Hello, my littlest angel," she cooed, and gave Bryn a big kiss. "Would you like to come help Grammy make soup for your mommy?"

Bryn jumped up and down and clapped her hands. "Yes!"

Suzanne searched her memory for a time Bryn had been that excited over doing something with her and came up empty. That was because her brain was fuddled with pain pills. Later she'd remember something. Wouldn't she?

THIRTEEN

The second time Suzanne awoke it was to the aroma of tomato and spices and the yeasty fragrance of home-baked bread. Those were the smells of her childhood and as comforting as the blankets she was nestled under. Her mother's taste in clothes and décor were abysmal, but when it came to cooking, Mary Madison could have had her own show on the Food Network.

Suzanne stretched and then reached for her cell phone only to find it was no longer on her nightstand. She checked to see if it had fallen on the floor. No cell phone there, either. She frowned. If Bryn had sneaked it away to play with she was going to be in big trouble.

Suzanne pushed herself off the bed and grabbed the instruments of torture known as crutches, and made her clumsy way to the upstairs hall. "Guy!"

Guy didn't come. Instead her mother appeared at the foot of the stairs. She had donned an apron over her polyester pants and

Bryn appeared at her side like a living accessory. "Oh, you're awake," she said.

Bryn detached herself and ran up the stairs, bearing a miniature marshmallow tower covered in pink sprinkles. "Look, Mommy. We made marshmallow snowmen."

Goody. The craft marathon had begun.

Bryn held it out for Suzanne to take.

Suzanne kissed her daughter and gave her a hug. "That's very nice, Brynnie."

"This one's for you. Try it, Mommy," urged Bryn, shoving it in front of her nose.

"I can't right now, baby," said Suzanne. *Thank God.* "Mommy needs to take her pain pills first. You keep it for me in the kitchen. Okay?" Her daughter's hands were a sticky mess. "And then go wash your hands before you touch anything."

Bryn made a face and trudged back down the stairs and Mom's brows took a disapproving dip.

Ah, how well Suzanne knew that expression. "Where's Guy?"

"I told him there was no need to hang around here when he had things to do," said Mom, "not when I can take over."

Take over was right. And Guy had been happy to let her. What was with that? Her husband just ran off and left her the minute the next shift arrived?

He has to work, her rational self reminded her, but she told it to shut up. "Do you know where my cell phone is?"

"Oh, I took it downstairs," said her mother as if it were perfectly acceptable to take someone's cell phone. "I figured you need your rest."

Suzanne could feel her blood pressure rising. "I've had my rest. Now I need my cell phone."

Her mother's easy smile stiffened. "Fine. I'll get it. Would you like some soup?"

"That would be great," said Suzanne, equally stiff. "Thanks."

There was nothing else to say after that, and besides, Suzanne's ankle was not happy. Scowling, she maneuvered herself back to her bedroom. By the time she got back to bed she was exhausted. This was so not fun. She grabbed her bottle of happy pills and popped one. At the rate things were going, by the time her mother left she'd be a drug addict.

Mom appeared a few minutes later, carrying a tray with a steaming bowl of soup and a plate with a slice of fresh-baked bread smothered in Suzanne's healthful butter-substitute spread. The aroma of tomato, garlic, and onions spread through the bedroom. Suzanne sniffed and closed her eyes. Just the smell made her feel better.

She opened her eyes as Mom set the tray on her lap. There, next to the bread, lay her cell phone. Good. She was connected to the outside world once more.

Mom perched on the foot of the bed. "How are you feeling?" Her tone of voice said, *Let's make up.*

Sick in bed with her mommy bringing soup; suddenly, Suzanne felt twelve years old again, and in need of understanding. "Crummy. Frustrated." She tested a spoonful of soup. "This is great," she said, and dipped the spoon back in, dredging up a pile of finely cut carrot, celery, and parsnip. Mom had given her this recipe last winter but she'd never gotten around to making it.

"You always did love that soup. Your daughter likes it, too," Mom added with a smile.

Suzanne bit into the bread. Wait a minute. This wasn't her spread. This was real butter. "You bought butter?"

"Real butter is better for you than that awful imitation stuff," said Mom.

"You went out and bought butter?" When had she found time for that?

"I brought a few things up with me," said Mom. "I figured if I was going to come up early for Christmas I might as well bring some ingredients for baking. I think Bryn will enjoy that."

"She'd like anything her grammy made," said Suzanne in an effort to be gracious. "I suppose she's been talking your ear off."

"A little." Mom smoothed the bedspread. "Mostly about a dog named Happy."

Suzanne shook her head. "That dog."

"She appears to have her heart set on it."

"Well, I have my heart set on a diamond necklace," Suzanne retorted. "That doesn't mean I'm going to get it."

"You're not a little girl," said her mother, with that same superior smile she always used when handing out unrequested advice. Before Suzanne could think of anything to say, she stood and moved away. "I'd better get downstairs and see what she's up to."

Suzanne let out her breath in an irritated hiss as her mother bustled her busybody self out of the room. Shouldn't she be at school still, bossing around helpless children? Two weeks of this. Suzanne would go crazy.

"I'm losing my mind," she told Allison when her friend called to check on her Saturday morning. "Julie is having to take my clients around, Bryn is making an army of marshmallow snowmen and expecting me to eat every one, and my mother is, well, my mother."

"Any time you want to trade moms let me know," said Allison, her voice taking on a scolding tone.

"How about now? I'll send her right over. She can help you make some more fudge."

"Deal," said Allison.

Suzanne could see Allison and Mom in Allison's state-of-the-art kitchen, whipping up exotic confections in Allison's designer pots. Those two had a mutual admiration society going. "Why don't you come over here for dinner tonight instead?" What the heck? Let Allison have a dose of Mom. It would give Suzanne a break.

"That sounds good to me."

"Great," said Suzanne. "I'll call Kiles, too." Like Allison was always reminding her, girlfriend time was important.

"Don't bother," said Allison. "She already got a better offer. She and Craig are going skating at the Lynnwood Ice Center and then out for pizza."

Kiley was going into this new relationship at a gallop, racing for another heartbreak. "Have you met this guy?" asked Suzanne.

"Actually, he came by when we were making fudge. He's funny and kind, perfect for her. It looks like that snow globe was the best investment Kiles ever made."

"Yeah, well, it sure paid off for me," Suzanne grumbled.

"If you don't want it, I'll take it."

"You can have it with my blessing." Right along with her mother. "Just don't sue me when it ruins your life."

They chatted a little longer. Then Allison went back to her baking for the holiday home tour and Suzanne returned to being bored.

Until she remembered that the decorators were finally coming. Yes! She threw off the bed covers. She was going downstairs no matter what.

Since it was Saturday Guy was on hand to help her clean up and get downstairs. But on hearing about the pending invasion, he took off for the gym. She had coffee and a piece of toast for breakfast and averted her eyes from the ratty snowman and snow lady Mom and Bryn were constructing from cotton batting.

"We thought they would look nice on the fireplace mantel, right next to the snow globe," said Mom. "Didn't we, Brynnie?" She smiled at Bryn who was happily gluing a lopsided eye on her snow lady.

"We'll see," said Suzanne noncommittally. "I've got the decorators coming today."

"Ah." Mom nodded, her politeness poorly masking her disapproval.

Too bad, thought Suzanne. This was her house, not her mother's.

To prove it she set up court in the living room and watched while the place became a thing of beauty. When the Holiday

Creations crew left a nine-foot tree graced the bay window, simply yet tastefully decked with gold balls and wine-colored ribbon and tiny white lights. The same theme was carried up the stair banister and along the mantel.

Suzanne made the circuit with her crutches, pleased with all she saw. Everything was perfect, from the front hall to the powder room. "It looks like we're ready for the holidays," she said happily as she swung her way back into the living room.

Bryn, who had been following the workers from room to room, looked at the mantel and frowned. "Where can we put our snowman and snow lady, Grammy?"

Suzanne's mother cocked an eyebrow at her. That eyebrow. Her mother always could say so much with it. Right now Suzanne didn't particularly like what she was saying.

"How about we put them on your dresser?" Suzanne suggested.

Bryn's lower lip stuck out. "But then nobody can see them."

That was the general idea.

"How about here?" Mom suggested, plopping the tacky things on the new coffee table, right next to the pillar candle arrangement. The perfect tacky finishing touch, and a fire hazard to boot.

"They might catch fire there," said Suzanne. Had her mother thought of that? Nooo. "I think your room would be better."

"But I want Aunt Kiley and Aunt Allison to see them," protested Bryn, frowning.

"They will," Suzanne assured her. "They'll come up to your room and look. And just think, you'll have your very own special Christmas room," she added. "You can put them right next to your pink Christmas tree, and you'll be able to look at them every night when you go to sleep."

Bryn gave up. "Okay." She hugged the ugly things to her and left the room, frowning.

Suzanne kept her gaze focused on her daughter, successfully avoiding visual contact with The Eyebrow. But she didn't escape The Sigh, which was almost as bad.

She turned to her mother and demanded, "What?"

"The house looks beautiful, dear. It really does. Certainly more lovely than anything you had growing up." Her mother stopped and bit her lip.

She was on a roll. Why stop now?

"But," prompted Suzanne. As if she didn't know what was coming next.

"I just think what makes a home truly beautiful is the happiness shared by the people who live in it."

"We're happy," Suzanne protested. How could they not be? "Our life is perfect."

"It certainly looks that way," said her mother. The sneaky little dig wasn't lost on Suzanne, but before she could respond, Mom said, "I think I'll get busy in the kitchen. If Allison's coming over she'll want Spritz Christmas tree cookies," then made her exit, leaving her daughter smarting.

The sting continued all day and into the evening, making it hard for Suzanne to appreciate her friend's visit. Guy had insisted on moving their daughter's craft project back down to the living room and the snow couple was now on the coffee table in place of the candles, sitting in judgment on Suzanne, and pronouncing her the world's worst mother. To top it all, Mom fussed over Allison as though she was the daughter Mom never had.

Finally, Suzanne had enough. "My ankle is hurting. I think I'm going to go to bed."

"Do you want help up the stairs?" Mom offered.

"You've helped enough for one day," Suzanne assured her.

"I'll help her," said Guy, getting up.

She would have appreciated his offer if his tone of voice hadn't added, *Pain in the butt that she is.* "I can manage," she said stiffly.

"Let your husband help you," said Mom. "That's what he's here for."

More unrequested advice. "Mom," Suzanne said sternly.

"You can pretend you're Scarlett O'Hara and he's Rhett Butler," quipped Allison in an attempt to lighten the moment.

"I can do it myself," Suzanne snapped.

Guy shrugged and said, "Okay then. Knock yourself out, babe."

Suzanne turned around in a huff and hobbled off.

By the time she got to her bedroom she had a thin film of sweat on her forehead and tears on her cheeks. No one understood her.

She managed in the bathroom, then popped a pain pill and fell into bed.

She had just gotten settled when her mother arrived with a cup of cocoa. She handed it over with an empathetic look. "I thought you could use this."

Mom always did think cocoa was the solution to all of life's problems. It had made Suzanne feel better when she was a child, but she wasn't a child now, even if she was acting like one.

"I know this isn't fun," her mother said gently, "but maybe there's a silver lining here. Maybe this is God's way of slowing you down a little."

Oh, that was helpful. "I don't need to slow down. I need to make money. This place doesn't maintain itself. It takes two salaries."

"I understand," said her mother.

What a joke. Their house growing up had been a hodge-podge of garage sale furniture and ugly, homemade decorations. Always a mess. Mom had never cared. She'd never even tried to improve the house. Instead she'd bumped along as if life was just fine as it was. Maybe for her, but not for her daughter. Suzanne still remembered having to make excuses for why she couldn't go on trips with her friends or to school dances when the truth was that there was no money in the budget for those extras. Was it so wrong for her to want to spare Bryn the same disappointments?

"No, you don't," Suzanne snapped. "I don't want to live like you."

She regretted the words the minute they were out of her mouth. They were true but they were also cruel. It was the pain pills; they were scrambling her brain.

Her mother turned to stone. "I know I couldn't provide you with the kind of elegant lifestyle some of your friends had, but really, was your life so bad, Suzanne? Our home wasn't full of expensive knickknacks but it was full of love. Which would you rather have had?"

Love, of course. Suzanne bit her lip.

"There's more to life than selling houses," her mother continued. "And there's certainly more to life than living in one that looks like something from a magazine layout. You're becoming so consumed with this place that you're starting to forget about the people who live in it. This isn't a dollhouse. Your husband and daughter are real people with real needs. And let me tell you, life is short. You can lose the people you love in a heartbeat. Now, drink your cocoa."

Suzanne scowled and set the cocoa on the nightstand as her mother left the room. She didn't want cocoa and she didn't want a lecture and she didn't want a broken ankle!

Even in sleep the torture continued. She dreamed that the angel flitted out of the snow globe and stood before her, an eight-foot tower in a glowing robe and a halo that looked suspiciously like Christmas lights. "You're a mess," she observed in disgust.

"Gee, thanks," Suzanne retorted. "It's your fault I'm like this, you know."

The angel rolled her eyes. "Oh, please."

"Is there a reason you're here?" Suzanne demanded.

"Yes, as a matter of fact, there is. I've come to show you your future. Look."

At first all Suzanne could see was mist. Then, slowly, it cleared and she made out a middle-aged, slightly overweight woman sitting in a living room decorated for the holidays. The décor could have been lifted from the pages of *Better Homes and Gardens.*

"Well, the house looks great," Suzanne said.

"It should. There's no one in it to mess it up," said the angel.

"What happened to me?" wondered Suzanne, regarding her plumper, older self in disgust. "When did I gain all that weight?"

"Menopause," said the angel. "And you were depressed."

"Why was I depressed? What happened?" Suzanne asked, and braced herself.

"Your husband left you. He remarried. She's a total slob."

The blow to both her heart and ego made Suzanne gasp. "You're kidding, right?"

The angel cocked an eyebrow. "Do you think angels kid about things like this?"

"Why did he leave? I don't understand."

"Oh, don't play dumb," snapped the angel, adjusting her halo. "Why do you think he left?"

Suzanne decided to plead the Fifth. "What about my daughter?" she asked in a small voice. "Where is she?"

"Look," the angel said with a sweep of her hand.

"Oh, good Lord," gasped Suzanne as the angel showed her a garish house laden with multicolored lights, its yard a dump for every plastic holiday decoration ever invented.

"Don't worry," said the angel. "You don't have to deal with it. She never invites you over. She never comes to see you, either. You're a pain in the butt."

Suzanne blinked in shock. "What kind of a way is that for an angel to talk?"

"The truth hurts," said the angel. "By the way, I brought you a present." She turned around and picked up something hiding behind her robe and Suzanne saw it was a dog, a grown version of Happy.

The dog jumped out of the angel's arms and ran over to Suzanne and chomped into her ankle with huge fangs.

Suzanne woke up with a strangled scream to a dark room. She was sitting up in her bed and Guy was next to her.

He sat up, too. "You all right, babe?"

Suzanne pushed her damp hair out of her eyes with a trembling hand. "It was awful. Bryn hated me and I was alone. And fat."

"You just had a nightmare. Everything's all right," he assured her, his voice heavy with sleep. He kissed the top of her head and then flopped back down and turned over on his side.

"Guy, am I a pain in the butt?"

"Sometimes," he mumbled, burying his head deeper in his pillow.

She leaned over him. "Would you leave me for a slob?"

"I wouldn't leave you for anything. Come on, babe, it's three in the morning. Let's go back to sleep," he added, easing her back down next to him.

"Guy, do you love me?"

"Of course I love you. Do you need another pain pill? Are you hurting?"

She was hurting, but it was nothing the pills on her night-stand could combat. "I'm fine," she lied. "Sorry I woke you."

"No problem," he said, and a moment later he was snoring.

But Suzanne lay in bed, wide awake, fearing that if she shut her eyes she'd fall back asleep and the angel would get her.

It gave her a lot of time to think.

By the time the first light of morning slipped past the bedroom curtains Suzanne had found a new attitude. Changes of heart were wonderful, she decided. She felt like a whole new woman, swathed in holiday warmth. This was going to be a truly perfect Christmas. She was going to make sure of it!

As soon as Guy went downstairs to help her mother with breakfast she grabbed her cell phone and called the Lovgrins, her heart racing with excitement. She barely gave April time to say hello. "We'd like to get Happy for Bryn for Christmas."

"Suzanne, I'm sorry," said April. "Happy was adopted yester-day.

FOURTEEN

Suzanne stared at her phone in disbelief. "Yesterday?" How could this be? What kind of sick angel appeared to someone in a dream a day late?

"You said you didn't want him," April reminded her.

"I know, but I changed my mind." Here she was, turning over a new leaf, and the Spirit of Christmas was rewarding her by dropping a Christmas tree on her head. That wasn't how it worked for Scrooge. Something was terribly, terribly wrong here. "Don't you have any dogs left?"

There was a moment of silence on the other end of the line. "Maybe it was just my imagination," said April at last, "but you didn't seem interested in a dog. In fact, I got the distinct impression you don't much like dogs."

"Man's best friend? What's not to like?" lied Suzanne. "Guy has had dogs all his life and you know Bryn is dying for one."

Another pregnant pause.

Suzanne rushed to fill it. "April, I've had a dog epiphany. Really. If you have any puppies left it would mean so much to all of us to be able to adopt one."

"We still have Hildy."

Hildy, Happy, who cared? As long as it was a dog. "Great," said Suzanne. "We'll take her."

"All right," April said, her tone of voice adding, *I hope I won't regret this.* "We'll get things rolling for you. By the way, how's the ankle?"

"It's getting better," said Suzanne. It had to, she thought, since after Christmas she was going to have a new baby to care for.

She'd barely hung up the phone when her mother entered the room, carrying a mug of coffee and a plate with freshly baked cinnamon rolls. Her smile looked a little forced and Suzanne felt the weight of all the mean things she'd said the night before. "You didn't have to bring me anything. I was going to come down."

"That's okay," said her mother, handing over the goodies. "I wanted a minute to talk alone."

That meant another lecture was coming for sure, but this one was well deserved. "I'm sorry I've been such a brat," Suzanne said earnestly. "And I'm sorry about what I said last night."

Her mother shook her head and laid a hand on Suzanne's arm. "No, I'm the one who needs to apologize. There's no shame in working to have nice things. God knows I gave you few enough."

Suzanne saw the glisten of tears in her mother's eyes and felt fresh guilt. When had she become so shallow? Surely she hadn't been born that way. She hugged her mother fiercely. "You gave us love and that was plenty." Why had she thought she needed more? Why had she felt such a burning desire to be just like her rich friends?

"Thank you, darling," Mom said, and kissed her cheek. "Now, about this holiday home tour. How can I help you?"

The holiday home tour was a smashing success. Suzanne parked herself, cast and all, at the house that served as the reception home, plying visitors with Allison's brownies and brochures while Mom helped Julie and two other agents from the office squire visitors from house to house. By the end of the day three of the agency's listings had offers on them. Suzanne's mother had cinched one of the deals by informing a pair of expectant parents that their child would thank them someday for giving her such a lovely home to grow up in. Of course, being Mom, she had also thrown in as a bonus a little lecture on how to have a happy home.

"Do you really believe what you told them about having a nice house?" Suzanne asked as her mother tooled them home in Suzanne's Lexus.

"Beauty is a subjective thing," she said with a shrug. "I could tell they were in love with the house. They simply needed someone to give them permission to buy it."

Mom was a natural. "Maybe you should forget teaching and go into real estate," said Suzanne.

Her mother shook her head. "No. I'm exactly where I want

to be. I like helping children learn and grow. And I like having time off at the holidays to be with my family," she added with a smile.

Actually, so did Suzanne.

When Christmas Eve came, Mom was in her element. Suzanne's brother, Loren, and his family ferried over from nearby Vashon Island and her mother stuffed them all to the gills with her famous Swedish meatballs. After the presents had been exchanged and Loren's family had left, she cleaned up the mess, restoring order to chaos, then led Bryn off for a bedtime story so Guy could steal away to fetch home the new puppy.

"I'd ask if you're going to be okay while I'm gone, but with your mom here that would be a dumb question," he said after he'd helped Suzanne upstairs. "Looks like her coming up early turned out not to be such a bad thing after all."

"It's worked out," Suzanne admitted.

"I'll say," agreed Guy, giving his stomach a satisfied pat. "Well, I'd better get going."

He gave her a quick kiss and started to leave but she caught his arm. "Remember when Bryn saw the puppy in the snow globe and you said you saw our house?"

"Yeah," he said slowly.

"Did you?"

Guy made a face. "Of course not. I was just playing along. I'll be back in half an hour."

Suzanne gave her lip a thoughtful chew as he left the room.

Had she imagined what she saw? She supposed it didn't really matter at this point.

She was settled in bed by the time Guy returned with the female version of Happy. He plopped the new baby on the bed.

"My spread!" protested Suzanne as the puppy bumbled its way to her.

"It'll be okay," Guy assured her.

Happy the Second clambered up Suzanne's chest to lick her face, nearly bowling her over with a strong dose of puppy breath.

"Someone needs an Altoid," Suzanne said, picking up the pup and holding her at arm's length.

The puppy wriggled in her hands, anxious to display affection.

"Yes, you're a good dog," Suzanne assured her. "Now go see Guy," she added, holding the dog out to him.

"Come here, you," Guy said. "Time to be in your crate." He cuddled the puppy to him much the way had cuddled Bryn when she was a baby.

The sight made Suzanne's heart catch. She had definitely done the right thing. But if the dog peed on her carpet . . .

Fortunately for Hildy-Happy, she didn't. And Bryn's ecstasy when she saw her father sitting at the foot of the tree on Christmas morning, the puppy in his arms, was worth more than a thousand ruined carpets.

"What a perfect present!" Allison exclaimed when she and Kiley stopped by on their way to their family celebrations. She picked the puppy up and it immediately went to work covering her neck and face in puppy kisses.

"No," said Suzanne, holding out a box wrapped in burgundy

paper and tied with an elaborate gold ribbon. "This is a perfect present. Open it."

Allison set the dog down and reached for the present. "Is this what I think it is?" she asked with an eager smile.

"It's your turn," said Kiley.

Allison ripped into the paper, making Suzanne wince. She lifted the lid and fished out the snow globe.

"Shake it," urged Kiley.

Allison hesitated a moment. Then she shook her head and nested it back in its tissue paper bed. "No. Not before I have to go to my parents. It would be bad luck."

"Oh, come on," urged Kiley. "It'll help you get through the day."

Allison pulled out the snow globe, and gave it a jiggle.

"Well?" prompted Kiley. "See anything?"

Allison looked like she was going to cry. Uh-oh, thought Suzanne, and exchanged a worried look with Kiley.

"It looks like my grandma," Allison said. "Not exactly, but close enough."

"What's she doing?" asked Suzanne.

"She's drinking tea with me." Allison closed her eyes and hugged the snow globe.

"Maybe the snow globe is giving you courage," Kiley suggested.

Allison opened her eyes and nodded. "Probably. God knows, with my family I'll need it."

"Speaking of family"—Kiley checked her watch—"I've got to get going. Craig and I have to be at my parents' by one."

The three friends exchanged their other presents and then Kiley and Allison left Suzanne and her family to enjoy their holiday meal and their new baby.

"Happy looks different," Bryn observed later as she and the dog settled on the couch with Suzanne while Guy and Mom did K.P.

Uh-oh. "How?" asked Suzanne, hoping her tired brain would be able to come up with a quick explanation, appropriate for a seven-year-old, to account for for Happy's missing body part.

"He looks happier," said Bryn, petting the puppy's head.

"That's because he's found a happy home," said Suzanne.

"I'm glad Santa didn't take him to Virginia," Bryn said in a tired voice as Suzanne stroked her hair.

"Me, too," murmured Suzanne.

A few moments later both Bryn and the new puppy were asleep, Bryn snuggled next to Suzanne and the exhausted dog curled up on Suzanne's lap.

It was the best Christmas she'd had in a long time, she decided as she gazed at the flame in the gas fireplace.

"Now, that's a perfect picture."

She looked up to see Guy leaning in the doorway and smiled back at him. "Merry Christmas. Have I told you lately that you're a great husband?"

He grinned. "You're just saying that because it's true." He grabbed his digital camera from the coffee table and recorded the moment, then turned the camera so Suzanne could see.

She didn't need to look, really. She'd already seen this scene, in the snow globe.

FIFTEEN

Allison carefully set the snow globe on the front seat of her car to ride shotgun as she drove to her parents' house.

"You came on the scene just in time," she muttered. "I could use some moral support."

If she hadn't broken up with Lamar the week before she could have been with his family, enjoying the holiday with sane people. But she'd finally realized she loved his mother and sister more than him—not the right reason to keep a man. So today all she had to look forward to was Christmas dinner at her father and stepmother's house. With no Grandma to ease the torture.

It's only two hours, she reminded herself, two hours out of your day, out of your life.

Except what usually happened during those two hours was enough to give her nightmares for the following eleven months. In the past she'd had her grandmother to balance out the chaos but this year she was on her own.

She pulled up in front of the modest brick rambler in Ballard and parked in back of a black Hummer. So her stepbrother, Joey, and his wife were already here. How long had everyone been whooping it up? More to the point, how much eggnog had been consumed?

She took a deep breath to steel herself, then got out of the car and took her red velvet cake and the shopping bag full of gifts from the backseat. Maybe she was worrying for nothing. Maybe it would be okay.

Oh, who was she kidding? The day was bound to be a disaster. Grandma had always held the reins of what was left of her daughter's family, keeping an eye on things in the kitchen, frowning and gently shaking her head when the partying started to get out of hand, discreetly monitoring the punch consumption. No one was holding the reins now.

The neighborhood was an old one, consisting mostly of smaller homes, many renovated, all worth a small fortune. Several houses were festooned with Christmas lights. Her stepmother had gotten right into the spirit of things. The house dripped icicle lights, and a fat wreath sporting candy canes and red bows hung on the front door. To look at the place you'd have thought June and Ward Cleaver lived inside. Looks could be deceiving.

Allison heard the noise even before she opened the front door. Joey was playing one of his favorite tacky Christmas songs at full blast, and over that she could hear raucous male laughter and the barking of a dog—Boozle, her father's bloodhound.

She took a deep breath and forced herself to open the door. Just in time to hear the crash of something breaking in the living room. She walked in to find her father, her stepbrother, and another man, obviously a friend of Joey's, staring at a broken floor lamp, which now lay in pieces on the wood floor along with a few dust bunnies. With their rock concert souvenir T-shirts and droopy, faded jeans, Joey and his friend looked like redneck twins.

Dad had dressed up for the day and was resplendent in slacks and a sweater so brightly red Allison almost needed sunglasses to look at him. "You've done it now, sport," he said to Joey with a shake of his head.

"It wasn't me," protested Joey. He gave his friend a shove. "Way to go, bigfoot."

Here was a case of the pot calling the kettle black. Joey was the size of a small nation, easily dwarfing his buddy, a thirty-something man with a receding hairline.

Now Allison's stepmother Sandi, Aunt Connie, and Joey's wife, Carissa, were in the living room. Sandi's dyed blond hair was already going limp and her face was flushed—hopefully from working in the kitchen and not from having sampled too much eggnog. She wore tight jeans to show off the fact that she'd recently lost five pounds and a sweater as insistently red as her husband's and trimmed with rhinestone-studded snowflakes.

"My lamp!" she cried, throwing up her hands. "What were you boys doing?"

"Just a little wrestling," said Joey.

Meanwhile, Boozle had spotted Allison and trotted over to greet her, jumping up on her with an excited bark.

"Down, Boozle," she commanded, struggling to push him away and keep a hold on her presents and the cake.

Joey's face lit up at the sight of Allison. "Hey, Sis. Long time no see." He walked over to her and gave her a playful punch in the shoulder, then checked out her leather jacket, jeans, and black turtleneck sweater, nodding appreciatively. "You look good. Lost weight?"

Yes, but she wasn't going to admit that in front of some stranger. She ignored the question, kissing her father, who swept her into a big bear hug with a "Merry Christmas, Allie."

Sandi pointed a finger at Joey. "Clean up that mess and no more wrestling." She broke off to welcome Allison with a kiss on the cheek. Yep, Sandi had already been in the eggnog.

Carissa fetched the broom and dustpan. She was a pretty woman, with auburn hair and big green eyes and a perfect figure, not to mention a great job. What she was doing with Joey, the king of the unemployment check, was a mystery to Allison. They'd gotten married right after high school, so maybe she just didn't know any better.

Meanwhile, Joey was already saying to his friend, "This is Allison. Didn't I tell you she's hot?"

The friend smiled sheepishly at Allison. "Hi. I'm Ed. I didn't break the lamp," he added.

Allison sighed inwardly. Two hours. Just two hours. She said a quick hi to Ed, then set her bag of gifts by the tree and kissed her Aunt Connie. When Allison was little she had thought Aunt Connie was a movie star—an easy mistake to make considering the fact that Aunt Connie had looked like Audrey Hepburn, slim, lovely, and well dressed. She'd lost her svelte figure when she gave up smoking, but never her taste in clothes.

Today her curves were concealed under an ensemble in classic lines and fashionable colors, and her dark hair, now shot with gray, was cut short and stylish. She wished Allison a merry Christmas and managed a sour smile.

Allison supposed she'd be sour too if she'd gone through two husbands and was reduced to spending Christmas with the flake who'd married her brother.

"I'll take the cake into the kitchen," Aunt Connie volunteered. She lifted the plastic container from Allison's hand and marched back to the kitchen, past a table made festive with Spode Christmas dishes that had belonged to Allison's mother. Someday they were supposed to go to Allison, but every year another piece got chipped or broken and she wasn't holding out much hope that there would be many pieces left by the time her stepmother got around to giving them to her. Sandi had cleaned off the dining room table for the occasion. It was usually piled high with the flotsam and jetsam of her life: department store coupons, magazines, plants that never quite made it to the garden, flavored Vodka from the liquor store—anything and everything. A good amount of the junk was now piled on top of the buffet, pretty much burying Mom's old silver service.

"Can I help?" asked Allison, following her aunt.

"You sure can. You can take the damned turkey out of the oven. It's been in there so long it looks like it belongs in Death Valley," snapped Aunt Connie. A pot on the stove started boiling over and she yanked it off the burner. "I told Sandi an hour ago it should come out, but would she listen? No."

Oh, it was going to be a long day. It was almost enough to

make Allison want to reach for the eggnog. Almost. Instead, she poured herself a glass of water and took a fortifying sip.

Sandi was in the kitchen now. "I'm just keeping it in there to stay warm, Connie. I told you that." Sandi shook her head. "She takes one cooking class at Shoreline and thinks she's Julia Child."

"Is that so?"

"Yes, it is. Now quit acting like you've got PMS. We all know you're too old," Sandi added with a wink at Allison. "We're going to open presents before dinner." She turned and led the way back to the living room where Carissa was sweeping the last bit of broken lamp into a dustpan. "Thank God we pulled up the carpet," Sandi said. "Hardwood makes cleanup so much easier."

Given the way things happened in their household, stainless-steel floors that could be hosed down would have been the best bet, if you asked Allison. What would their family have been like if her mother had lived? Surely not this.

All the furniture had been arranged to face the artificial fiber optics tree, a vision in changing colors and Hallmark collectible ornaments. Everyone settled in with a cup of eggnog or beer bottle in hand. Boozle settled on Allison's feet.

Allison wrinkled her nose. The room smelled of pine-scented candle, male sweat, and . . . oh, yuck, what had they fed Boozle? Allison removed her feet from under the dog's hindquarters and relocated to the sofa. Sitting next to Aunt Connie beat the heck out of smelling Boozle.

Dad played Santa, passing around presents. "Here's a big one for you, Sis," he said to Aunt Connie, handing her a shirt box. Wonder what it is."

"An inflatable man," said Sandi, and snickered at her cleverness.

"I don't need a man to feel good about myself," Aunt Connie informed her. "Unlike *some* people."

Meanwhile, in the background the radio station Sandi had found was playing "We Need a Little Christmas."

"Hey," said Dad, distracting Sandi by jiggling one of Allison's presents at her. "I'll bet there's something good to eat in here."

"Oh my God, my hips," protested Sandi, rolling her eyes.

Aunt Connie removed the lid from her box and pulled out a hideous, multicolored sweater. "This is a 2X. I don't wear a 2X."

"Oh, I thought I had the right size," Sandi said, opening her present. "You can return it." To Allison she said, "Thanks, Allie, but I'm on a strict holiday diet." She handed Allison back the tin of fudge.

Allison looked down at the sad little tin she'd carefully put together. What kind of person gave back a Christmas present because they didn't like it? Sandi could at least pretend to like it and then regift it later. That was proper Christmas etiquette, wasn't it?

"Well, I'll take it if she doesn't want it," said Joey, snatching it out of Allison's hands. He pulled off the lid and dove in.

Now Sandi was pulling the wrapping off a large box, joking, "This is one big bottle of perfume." As the wrapping fell away it became plain to see that it didn't hold another box that might eventually lead to a small perfume box. Instead, it was . . .

"A Thigh Master!" Sandi cried in disgust. If looks could kill, Dad would have been as dead as the Death Valley turkey waiting in the oven. "You got me a Thigh Master?"

Dad's round face lost its anticipatory smile. "You said you were unhappy with your thighs."

Sandi looked at him like he was insane. "So?"

"Well, I saw this on eBay and I thought you'd like it."

"It's used?" Sandi said in disgust. "You bought me a *used* Thigh Master for Christmas? I wanted perfume and you bought me a used Thigh Master!"

"Okay, fine," Dad said with a scowl. "I'll put it back up on eBay and get you some perfume."

"And you'd better not go looking for it on eBay," Sandi snarled.

Dad snatched a box out from under the tree with so much force the tree did a frantic hula. "Here, Allie, this is for you."

"From your Dad and me," added Sandi.

"Thanks," Allison said. She knew she didn't exactly sound excited, but so what? Sandi hadn't been excited about the fudge. *Well, what did you expect*, she scolded herself, *that your stepmother would suddenly become your best friend?*

She opened the box and pulled out a stack of books: *How to Succeed with Men; If I'm So Wonderful, Why Am I Still Single?; Dating for Dummies.*"

"*Dating for Dummies*. Ha! That's a good one," said Joey, reading over her shoulder.

She picked up the last book. *Stop Getting Dumped!* "I didn't get dumped," she protested.

But Sandi was too busy pouring herself another cup of eggnog to notice. Allison ground her teeth.

They should have been close. Sandi had wanted a daughter, or so she'd said, and Allison had needed a mother. What they'd each gotten instead was a rival, and the disconnect was complete when Sandi realized that the child she'd inherited would rather be a spectator and a homebody than a cheerleader, a caterer instead of a party girl. And now, apparently, someone who was destined to be a love reject.

"A secondhand Thigh Master," Sandi was muttering. "Who on earth gets his wife a used Thigh Master for Christmas?"

Dad was now looking distinctly uncomfortable. Tomorrow they'd be in the mall and he'd be making amends.

Allison watched as Sandi took a healthy slug of eggnog and then slammed it down on the coffee table with an angry slosh. *Are we having fun yet?*

SIXTEEN

The opening of presents turned more rowdy as the afternoon wore on. The men laughed uproariously over such treasures as a beer-toting reindeer that sang "Grandma Got Run Over by a Reindeer." Dad, the outdoorsman, was given slippers shaped like a trout, complete with glass eyes.

Aunt Connie gave Sandi a kitchen timer, starting fresh hostilities.

"I have a timer on my stove, Connie," Sandi said, her jaw tight and her eyes narrowed.

"You might have an easier time working this one," Connie said with artificial sweetness.

"Oh, that's funny," Sandi snapped as a chorus crooned "Silent Night" over the radio. *All is calm; all is bright.*

Not for long, thought Allison nervously. Aunt Connie's tongue and Sandi's temper—they mixed as well as oil and water.

"We've got to get going," said Carissa, standing. Carissa always knew when to scram.

Allison looked at her watch. Okay. It had been long enough. She could scram, too. "Actually . . ." she began.

"Aw, no." Dad protested. "We've got to have dinner. Sandi went to a lot of trouble."

"We have to get to my parents'," Carissa said firmly.

"Come on Rissa," said Joey. "We've got time for some turkey."

"We're having turkey with my family," Carissa said.

"Well, we can have some here, too," Joey decided. "Can't leave old Ed here by himself." He gave his friend a playful shove that almost sent Ed off the couch and toppling into the tree.

Carissa didn't seem to care about Ed. She was already giving Sandi a goodbye kiss on the cheek.

"Oh, stay a little longer, honey," begged Sandi. "We hate to see you run off."

"They'll probably be the only ones who don't get poisoned," Aunt Connie predicted under her breath.

She was drowned out by Joey booming, "I'm not ready to go anywhere. I told you I want to eat here at my parents' first. Now, we had this all decided."

Or at least Joey had.

"Sorry," Carissa said to Sandi, "we really do have to go. I thought we'd be eating sooner."

"Well, I'm not going," said Joey, crossing his arms in a show of manly independence. It might have been easier to take him seriously if he hadn't hiccupped.

"Suit yourself," said Carissa. "I'll see you back at the apartment."

"Now, wait just a damned minute." Joey jumped up, listing

a little in the process. He reached out to steady himself, catching a handful of Christmas tree and tipping the thing into the wall.

"Joey!" cried Sandi. "Be careful."

He righted himself after trampling two shirt boxes, and gingerly put the tree back in place. Meanwhile, Carissa was already putting on her coat. "You can't leave!" he hollered at her.

"Yes, I can," she yelled back. "I've got the car keys."

"How the hell am I supposed to get home?" he demanded.

"Ed can drive you. You're too drunk to drive anyway." Carissa glared at him. "And you promised you'd only have two beers."

"Looks like someone's sleeping on the couch tonight," predicted Dad in a pathetic attempt to cut the tension.

"Right along with you," snapped Sandi, making him scowl.

"Ha!" bellowed Joey. "Lately I've slept on the damned couch more than in my own bed."

"Thank you for sharing," said Aunt Connie sarcastically while Ed sat hunched on the couch, staring at his feet, probably wishing he were elsewhere.

Allison sure wished she was.

"I may as well become a monk for all the love you show me these days," Joey yelled at Carissa.

Carissa's face turned Christmas-stocking red. "Maybe I'd show you some love if you weren't a sweaty, unshaved, beer-breath slob. Ever think about that?"

Joey burped in response.

"I'm this close to filing for divorce, Joey." She held up two fingers an inch apart. "Go ahead and push me."

"Kids," shouted Dad. "Come on, now. It's Christmas."

Joey crossed his arms. "She called me a sweaty slob."

Carissa had resumed her march to the front door. "Go ahead. Stay here and drink yourself senseless. I have a real party to go to."

Joey gave her the old one-finger salute. "I didn't want to hang out with her family anyway," he announced as the front door slammed shut. "They're all boring. Boring!" he added at the top of his voice as if Carissa could hear him all the way out on the street. Maybe she could.

Right now boring sounded wonderful to Allison.

For a moment an awkward silence hung over the room. Dad broke it, rubbing his hands together and proclaiming heartily, "Well, I'm hungry. When's dinner, hon?"

"About two hours ago," said Aunt Connie.

"Oh, for God's sake," grumbled Sandi. She left her chair and started for the kitchen.

"I'll help you," said Aunt Connie grimly.

This meant World War Three was right around the corner. Allison longed to stay rooted to her chair, or, better yet, follow Carissa to safety, but it seemed wrong to let hostilities erupt without doing anything to try and stop them. "I'll help, too," she decided, and reluctantly followed her stepmother and aunt to the kitchen.

She left Joey on his cell phone yelling at Carissa for ruining Christmas.

"Son, watch the tree," Dad cautioned. "Boozle, no! Don't eat that! Joey, grab the fudge. Why'd you put it on the floor anyway? Watch the tree!"

From the dining room Allison heard a whoosh of branches scraping against the wall and the soft crunch of breaking ornaments but decided not to look. She knew she'd already have enough to deal with in the kitchen.

She arrived in time to see that the turkey was now out of the oven. Aunt Connie had been right. It should have come out hours ago.

"I told you," Aunt Connie was saying.

"It will be fine," Sandi insisted. "Just take the rolls out of the package and put them in the bowl."

So much for Grandma's biscuit recipe.

Aunt Connie looked shocked. "You don't want to heat them up first?"

"Okay, heat them up. I don't care." Sandi threw up her hands. "Why do we always have to do the holidays here?" she wailed. "I wish my mother-in-law was alive," she added, and began to cry.

Connie's hard exterior crumbled at that and she actually came over and put an arm around Sandi's shoulder. "It'll be okay. We'll get through it."

There was hope for world peace. Allison smiled.

"Now," Aunt Connie said briskly, "Allison, why don't you put the peas in the microwave and I'll mash the potatoes."

"I'll make the gravy," Sandi said with a sniff.

"Do you want me to do that?" asked Connie.

"No. I can handle it."

Allison wasn't so sure as she watched her stepmother slosh drippings from the turkey pan into a large skillet. Some of the drippings made it in, but more landed on the burner. Oh, that didn't look good.

"Um, Sandi, I can do that," Allison offered.

"I've got it," Sandi snapped, and cranked up the burner.

This started a cozy grease fire on the stovetop.

Sandi let out a surprised squeal and grabbed the half-consumed glass of water Allison had left behind on the counter. Allison and Aunt Connie both cried, "No!" just as she threw the water on the fire.

With a spatter and a demonic hiss, the flame spread like some special effect in a magic show, making Sandi jump back with a howl. "Fire!" she shrieked. "Oh, my God, we're on fire!"

"Where's the baking soda?" Aunt Connie demanded, diving for a cupboard.

Dad was in the kitchen now with Joey right behind him. "What's going . . . oh, my God!"

Now the flames were licking at the wall behind the stove and one of the side counters. The radio was blasting "There's No Place Like Home for the Holidays."

"Joe, get the fire extinguisher," barked Dad. "Girls, get out of the kitchen!"

He didn't have to ask Sandi twice. She was already on her way, screaming like her hair was on fire. It was a wonder it wasn't.

Allison would have followed her but now Ed was blocking the doorway, gawking, and Joey was running back in with the fire extinguisher. Meanwhile, Aunt Connie was pulling things out of the cupboards like a cop with a search warrant, muttering, "We just need baking soda."

Dad swept her aside with a mighty arm. "Get out of the way, Connie." He turned off the burner, then grabbed the fire extinguisher from his son and aimed, spewing a white stream at the stove.

A moment later everything was covered with gook and the kitchen smelled like a toxic dump. As for the turkey, it lay buried under a drift of chemicals. For a moment, everyone stood in silent awe, while from the living room a holiday chorus crooned, "Let it snow, let it snow, let it snow."

"Well," said Joey, "there went dinner."

SEVENTEEN

Allison had been so young when her mother died she barely remembered her. Dad, Grandma always said, was a bad boy with a good heart. He gave up his bad-boy ways when he married Allison's mother, and their life was like a storybook romance up until the day her mother died. Then her father returned to being a bad boy.

But Allison's grandmother had been a constant: the resident babysitter when Dad came out of mourning and decided to date (his euphemism for hitting bars and chasing bimbos). She'd also been the chauffeur, the sharer of Nancy Drew and Babysitter Club adventures, the keeper of secrets, and the queen of the kitchen. Allison's favorite after-school haunt had been her grandmother's house, located a convenient four blocks from home. In its sunny kitchen she had learned the art of making pie crust ("Don't handle it too much, dear. It makes the crust tough"), and the secret to fluffy biscuits ("Always use half cake flour, and add an egg"). With her grandmother so close by it

hadn't felt strange to live in a home with only echoes of femi-
ninity left behind from her mother. Before Sandi came on the
scene her father often took Allison fishing, but she never complained when he went hunting with his buddies and left her at
her grandmother's, a bastion of doilies, pretty knickknacks, and
kitchen gadgets. When she was older and found herself over-
whelmed by Joey's teasing and Sandi's lack of interest, she could
always run to her grandmother. And when she decided to try
catering for Suzanne's events her grandmother had given her a
gift certificate to their favorite kitchen shop by the Pike Place
Market so she'd have the best possible tools. She was an ace
baker and confectioner and the fudge she had made this year was
her best ever. Now Grandma, the one person who really understood and cared, wasn't around to share it. Except you still have
your memories of her, Allison reminded herself as she drove away
from the scene of Christmas carnage.

It was a relief to return to the little house that had been her
grandmother's. It was hers now, free and clear. She'd updated
the kitchen, making it state of the art, but the rest of the house
she'd kept pretty much the way it had been when Grandma was
alive, taking comfort in the antiques and vintage decorations.
Her pretty Christmas tree sat in the bay window, decked out
with fat, colored bulbs and blown-glass ornaments. The scene
was set for a perfect holiday.

She turned up the heat, hung up her coat, and then settled
on the couch with a cup of peppermint tea and the snow globe.
"You weren't much help today," she told it. She idly shook it,
watching the flakes swirl. When it settled to reveal the same

scene it had showed her earlier, Allison sighed and set it aside. Maybe it was broken. Maybe it would like to go home to Mrs. Ackerman.

She looked out the window. This had been one of the worst Christmases ever. Where were the grandma and the tea service that the snow globe had promised her?

She could almost hear her grandmother whispering in her ear, "Life is what you make it, dear. Sometimes you have to go find your happiness."

She tapped her cup thoughtfully. What could she make the rest of this day into?

She left the couch and wandered toward the one room where she'd always found happiness: the kitchen. Moving on autopilot she pulled out measuring cups and spoons, one of Grandma's old Pyrex nesting bowls, and her favorite mixing spoon. And smiled. Happiness wasn't that hard to find when you looked in the right place.

Half an hour later the kitchen smelled of melted chocolate, and the scent of almond extract danced in her nostrils. Another hour and she had a platter filled with cookies. She covered it loosely with foil, then went to fetch her coat and car keys.

The Grace Olsen House was dressed up for the holidays with swags in the windows and an artificial tree in the reception area, but these festive efforts couldn't overcome the pungent smell of urine and cleaning solution that crept along its vinyl floors. A few visitors strolled the halls, pushing old ladies in wheelchairs, but for the most part, residents lay on beds in their rooms alone or sat slumped in chairs here and there like vacant-eyed sentinels guarding the past.

One woman with wispy white hair and faded blue eyes to match her faded dress held out a clawed hand to Allison as she passed and croaked, "Help me."

Mrs. Manning. She'd been calling for help ever since Allison started visiting here.

Allison stopped and took a cookie from the platter. "Merry Christmas, Mrs. Manning," she said, and slipped the cookie into the woman's hand.

Mrs. Manning took a bite of the cookie and looked past Allison, possibly at the Ghost of Christmas Past. "You can't leave yet. The bird's not done."

Allison gave her arm a pat and kept going. She turned down the hall and went to a different wing. There was still vinyl on the floor here, and the same pungent smell followed her, but the rooms were bigger. They all looked out on the lawn and held a bed, a dresser, and a chair.

She ducked into room number 112, knocking on the door as she entered. A plump, little woman in a pink bathrobe sat in a chair by the bed, a book in her lap. She looked up curiously at the sight of Allison. Someone had brushed her hair today. Maybe her daughter had been in.

"Hi, Mrs. Baker," said Allison, coming into the room.

Her grandmother's old friend smiled at her tentatively. "Hello. Are you my daughter?"

Okay, not one of Mrs. Baker's good days. "No, I'm Allison. You and my grandma were best friends."

Mrs. Baker smiled. "Oh, were we? Who was your grandmother?"

Allison blinked back tears. This had been a stupid idea. "How about a cookie?"

"I love cookies," said Mrs. Baker, helping herself to one with a trembling hand. "You know, I won a baking contest once. I won a pink Sunbeam Mixmaster." She suddenly looked confused. "Do you still have it, Babs?"

"Yes," lied Allison. "I still do, and I love it."

Mrs. Baker smiled and took a bite of her cookie. "These are delicious." She stared at Allison, her brows knit. "What did you say your name was?"

"Babs."

Mrs. Baker smiled and shut her eyes. "It's nice to have company."

"Yes, it is," agreed Allison.

Some church group was caroling their way down the hall now, singing "We Wish You a Merry Christmas."

It was a little too late for that, but who knew? Maybe the new year would be happy. One could always hope.

EIGHTEEN

The new year brought new adventures. Kiley got engaged and Suzanne got pregnant. The year started well for Allison, too, who received a good review at work and a small raise. She never got what she saw in the snow globe, though.

"You know what I want to do," Kiley said as the three friends sat in Allison's kitchen, sipping tea and sampling Allison's new scone recipe. "I want to go see Mrs. Ackerman."

"Mrs. who?" asked Suzanne.

"Mrs. Ackerman, the woman who owned the snow globe before I bought it at the antique shop. I want to thank her and tell her everything that's happened. I think she'd like to hear that her family heirloom helped us."

Most of us, thought Allison, being careful to keep her expression neutral. She'd voiced her doubts once to Suzanne and had immediately regretted it. Suzanne now had all the zeal of a reformed cynic and she'd been quick to defend the powers of the snow globe. "You have to give it time," she'd insisted.

January was over now. As far as Allison was concerned, time had run out.

"Not a bad idea," Suzanne was saying. "If you want, I'll go with you."

They both looked at Allison.

That was what she wanted, to spend an afternoon listening to her two friends gush about the powers of the snow globe while she sat there like a holiday dud with no story to tell. "I don't think I can get away," she began.

"Oh, come on," pleaded Kiley. "We'll go on a weekend."

"It'll be fun," added Suzanne. She turned to Kiley. "See if you can track Mrs. Ackerman down and ask her if we can come this Saturday."

And just like that they were off and planning, assuming that Allison would come along. She frowned into her teacup. No way was she going.

Saturday was gray and blowy, and Allison looked like a thundercloud as the little ferry to Fawn Island dipped and rolled its way across a choppy Puget Sound. "I'm going to be sick," she predicted, crossing her arms over her down vest and scowling out the window at the sea of whitecaps.

"Stop pouting," Suzanne scolded. "I'm surviving and I feel like crap."

You could have fooled Allison. Suzanne looked totally put together in trouser jeans and a great jacket with a faux fur collar. And she was positively glowing. If that was what morning sickness looked like, where did a girl sign up?

"Anyway, you know you didn't want to be left behind," Suz added.

"Yes, I did," snapped Allison. She had no Christmas miracle to report, no good news. All she had was the snow globe, which had obviously run out of steam. Maybe Mrs. Ackerman would like it back.

"It'll be fun," Kiley promised. She crossed her booted legs and admired the engagement bling on her left hand.

"For you two," Allison said bitterly. All she was bringing into the new year was five extra pounds she'd gained after a post-Christmas cookie binge.

Suzanne shook her head. "You're becoming a real Scrooge."

"Who knows?" Kiley quickly put in. "This woman may have some great antiques. And you love antiques."

Allison loved her grandmother's antiques. There was a difference.

"Arriving Fawn Island," a voice announced over the loudspeaker. "All passengers must disembark. All car passengers please return to the car deck at this time."

"That's us," said Kiley cheerfully. "Let's go."

Suzanne hobbled off toward the exit, Kiley falling in next to her and allowing Allison to follow. This was a dumb idea. She wished she hadn't come. What was she going to say to Mrs. Ackerman, anyway? *Hi. I'm Allison and your snow globe hates me.*

She settled in the backseat of Kiley's car, thinking how appropriate it was that she was there like a third wheel. The two blessed ones sat up front, casually chatting, a road of promise stretching out before them. All she had back here in the loser's section was a good case of grumpiness.

They drove off the boat and through the quaint downtown, then, following the directions Kiley had written, turned onto a residential street, passing Cape Cod and Craftsman-style homes snugged in among fir trees and well-tended gardens with picket fences. Toward the edge of town, they came to a large, gray Victorian set high on the bluff overlooking the water.

"This is it," said Suzanne, and Allison's stomach clenched.

The paint was faded, but the yard was well tended, the flower beds weeded, and the rosebushes trimmed and waiting for spring. "This place would fetch a pretty penny," Suzanne mused as they went up the front walk.

They weren't even to the door yet when it opened, framing an elderly woman in a black dress and a European-style red wool jacket with gold braiding and buttons. She was short and stout, and wore glasses, and her white hair was elegantly styled.

"Welcome, ladies!" she called. "I'm Rosamunde Ackerman."

Allison hung back during the flurry of greetings, tongue-tied, clutching the snow globe for dear life.

"And this is Allison," Kiley added.

Mrs. Ackerman held out a hand. "Welcome, dear."

"Thanks," Allison managed. She took Mrs. Ackerman's extended hand. It was plump and dotted with age spots like

Grandma's had been. Allison swallowed down a bittersweet lump in her throat.

"I'm so delighted to have a chance to meet you all," said Mrs. Ackerman, ushering them into a living room thick with old furniture decked out in antimacassars. Everything smelled faintly of mothballs and lavender. In one corner of the room, an old brass birdcage housed a blue parakeet that hopped from perch to perch in excitement. Allison had seen that birdcage before. She'd seen this all. Her heart began to beat in time with the flitting bird.

"You just make yourselves at home," said Mrs. Ackerman. "I'll bring the tea."

"Let me help you," offered Allison.

The woman smiled at her. "Why, thank you."

In the kitchen, Allison took in the old Formica table like the one she owned now, the one that had been her grandmother's, the white shelf displaying Quimper plates and an antique brass teapot, the vintage mixer on the counter, and felt contentment settle in her chest. "This is lovely."

"Oh, I'm afraid it's all out of date," said Mrs. Ackerman with a sad smile. "Just like me."

"You don't have a daughter who's into antiques?" asked Allison.

"I don't have a daughter," said Mrs. Ackerman. "And I'm sad to say I lost my son in Vietnam." Her eyes took on a faraway look and Allison suspected she was envisioning happier times when her son was alive. She returned to the present with a little shake of her head and motioned to a china pot sitting on the counter next to the old stove. "I put the kettle on already. Perhaps you wouldn't mind pouring the water into the teapot."

"Not at all," Allison said with a smile.

They worked companionably, assembling cookies on a plate, fixing the teapot and teacups on a serving tray. Soon all was ready. Mrs. Ackerman took the plate of cookies out to the living room and Allison followed with the tray.

"Your house is lovely," said Suzanne.

"Yes, but it's a lot of house for one woman to rattle around in."

Suzanne perked up. "Have you ever thought of selling?"

"Maybe someday, but I'm not ready to leave behind my memories just yet," the old woman said with a smile that tugged at Allison's heartstrings. "Not that I'm complaining, mind you. I have my church and my wonderful neighbors." Her voice trailed off.

And no husband and no children, thought Allison sadly.

"But let's not talk about me," Mrs. Ackerman said briskly. "Tell me about the snow globe." She reached for the teapot with a shaky hand.

"Let me," said Allison.

She picked it up and poured tea while Kiley launched into her story. Mrs. Ackerman sat enthralled, never touching her cup.

Suzanne went next. "Who knew breaking my ankle would turn out to be good for my health?" she joked in conclusion, and Mrs. Ackerman chuckled.

Then the old woman turned to Allison. "And what about you, my dear?"

"She saw something in it at my house," said Suzanne, "but so far . . ."

"I saw you," Allison blurted. I saw this room and this teapot, and we were drinking tea, just like we are now. It almost looked like Grandma, but it was you. It was definitely you."

"I knew it would come through for you," Suzanne crowed, pointing a finger at her.

Then all three friends were talking at once, explaining how much Allison's grandmother had meant to her and how she'd served as a counterbalance to Allison's flaky family.

Mrs. Ackerman stirred cream into her tea. "Well," she said thoughtfully, "I've always said there are two kinds of family. There's the family of your flesh, and the one of your heart. One builds character, the other rewards it." She smiled at Allison.

Allison felt tears prickling her eyes. "If you're my reward, Mrs. Ackerman, I'll take it."

"Why, thank you, my dear," said the old woman.

They stayed another half hour, until it became clear that their hostess was getting tired. "We'd better go," said Kiley.

"First, we'll clean up, though," said Allison.

"Oh, that's not necessary," protested Mrs. Ackerman, but she didn't put up too much resistance when Kiley and Allison scooped up the tea things and took them to the kitchen to wash.

They were about to leave when Allison held out the snow globe to the old woman. "Would you like to have this back? It's obviously served its purpose for us."

Mrs. Ackerman smiled and shook her head. "As it has for me. No, you take it with you. I'm sure you'll find something to do with it." She hugged Allison. "And do come see me again."

As if she had to ask.

An hour later the three friends were back on the ferryboat, sailing home over waters much less troubled than when they came. A sliver of sunlight slipped through the gray skies and seagulls soared alongside the ferry, providing a feathered escort.

Allison studied the snow globe in her lap. "So, do you think this thing is like Aladdin's lamp?"

Suzanne shrugged. "I don't know about that. I sure never would have wished to break my ankle."

"Yes, but look at what you got," said Kiley with a smile.

Suzanne shrugged. "So maybe it's more a window meant to show you possibilities."

"I don't know," said Allison, running a hand over the treasure. "One thing I do know. We can't keep it."

"You're right, of course," Kiley said.

"Are you two insane?" Suzanne protested. "We need to hang on to it, pass it on to our kids. It's an heirloom."

"I'd say it's more than that," said Kiley.

"You can't just give it away," Suzanne said sternly. "Mrs. Ackerman would never approve."

"Actually, I think she would," said Allison. "After all, she told us to put it to good use."

"So, what should we do with it?" asked Kiley.

"You decide, Kiles," said Allison. "You're the one who found it."

Kiley chewed her lip thoughtfully for a moment, then said, "Leave it here."

Suzanne stared at her in disbelief. "Here? For just anyone?"

The three women looked around, taking in their fellow passengers. Over by the vending machines a harried mother was trying to corral a rambunctious preschooler and a toddler simultaneously. An elderly couple sat a few benches down, side by side in silence, staring out the window at the seagulls swooping over the waves. A sad-faced ferry worker slowly collected leftover newspapers for the recycling bin. A middle-aged woman hurried past, towing a beat-up carry-on suitcase.

"No," said Kiley. "For the right someone."

"Arriving Seattle," said the voice over the loudspeaker. "All passengers must disembark. Car passengers please return to the car deck at this time."

Kiley stood. "The snow globe found us. I think we can trust that it will find its way to the next person who needs it." She started for the car deck without so much as a backward glance.

Suzanne heaved a long-suffering sigh and followed her.

Allison took one last look around and then set the snow globe on the bench. Then, inspired, she fished a pad from her purse, tore off a piece of paper, and scrawled a note.

> *This is for someone who needs a miracle.*
> *If that's you, please take it.*

She smiled as she read what she'd written. Then she set the paper under the snow globe and hurried after her friends. It was going to be a great new year for someone.